Robert Langton

The Childhood and Youth of Charles Dickens

Robert Langton

The Childhood and Youth of Charles Dickens

ISBN/EAN: 9783337367268

Printed in Europe, USA, Canada, Australia, Japan

Cover: Foto ©Raphael Reischuk / pixelio.de

More available books at **www.hansebooks.com**

THE

CHILDHOOD AND YOUTH

OF

CHARLES DICKENS.

WITH RETROSPECTIVE NOTES, AND ELUCIDATIONS,
FROM HIS BOOKS AND LETTERS.

BY

ROBERT LANGTON,

F. R. Hist. Soc.,

Member of the Council of the Lancashire and Cheshire
Antiquarian Society.

LONDON :

HUTCHINSON & CO.,

25, PATERNOSTER SQUARE.

1891.

TO

MARY (MAMIE) DICKENS

AND

GEORGINA HOGARTH

[THE EDITORS OF THE *Letters of Charles Dickens*]

THIS BOOK IS INSCRIBED WITH THE UNAFFECTED

ADMIRATION AND REGARDS

OF THE WRITER.

PREFACE

TO ENLARGED AND REVISED EDITION.

--

IN 1883 a small edition of this book (for subscribers only) was issued privately.

Since that time many new and interesting facts have come to my knowledge, all of them tending to confirm the opinion then expressed, as to the close connection between the works of Charles Dickens and his own LIFE, and tending especially to show how his earlier experiences and surroundings, were coloured and reflected in his books.

· Of the new matter (dispersed through the book) much is taken into the text, the remainder is in footnotes. A few additional engravings have also been added.

It is a saddening thought, that of the friends

who helped me with the first edition, and whose names appear in the original Preface, far more than half have been removed by Death, in the few years that have since elapsed. Of these two or three only are mentioned in footnotes.

R. L.

December 3rd, 1890.

CONTENTS.

LIST OF ILLUSTRATIONS.

"God help all who turn to the Jerusalem of their younger days, and have an altar-fire upon the cold hearth of their fathers."—*American Notes*, Chap. VI.

"I have always observed within my experience, that the men who have left home young have, many long years afterwards, had the tenderest love for it, and for all associated with it. That's a pleasant thing to think of, as one of the wise and benevolent adjustments in these lives of ours."—*Letter to Hon. Mrs. Watson*, October 7th, 1856.

PREFACE

TO SUBSCRIBERS' EDITION.

FEW words of explanation may be necessary in introducing the following pages to my readers. About Midsummer, 1879, in consequence of a conversation with my friend, Mr. J. C. Lockhart, the Treasurer of the Manchester Literary Club, I promised to do what I could to produce and read

b

during the next Session of the Club, an essay on Charles Dickens and his connection with Rochester.

Following up this idea, in the August following I went to Rochester in company with the late Mr. William Hull, in order to make sketches to illustrate the paper. That paper was duly read and printed in the Club volume for 1880, and was afterwards enlarged, reprinted, and published by Messrs. Chapman and Hall.

Since that time I have had so many valuable and voluntary communications, containing hints and new facts on this most interesting subject, that I determined to widen the scope of the work, and instead of bringing out a third edition of my pamphlet,[1] to try how far I could give a sketch of the life of Charles Dickens from childhood up to youth and early manhood.

The work has grown upon me, and I have in the present volume not only utilised all the illustrations to the smaller book, but have in addition engraved from original and other drawings more than sixty new subjects. The biographical portion of this volume is on the lines of the early part of Mr. Forster's *Life of Charles Dickens*, and could not well have been otherwise, for without Mr. Forster's book I should have been working in the dark ; could not, indeed, in this connection, have worked at all !

[1] Up to this time (1889) five editions of this little work, *Charles Dickens and Rochester*, have been published.

It will, however, at once be apparent that many of my facts are totally at variance with Mr. Forster s text, and consequently at variance, too, with the numerous writers who have followed in his steps. It will also be seen that there is much that is quite new, and especially so during the early years at Chatham.

My thanks are due for valuable assistance to the following ladies and gentlemen, viz., Mrs. Andrews (Bexley Heath), Mrs. Austin (sister of Charles Dickens), Mr. Stephen T. Aveling, Mr. John Barksby, Mr. Jno. W. Bowden, Major and Mrs. Budden, Mr. Charles Bullard, Mr. L. Biden, F.R.H.S., Mr. John Brooker, Dr. Henry Danson, Mr. C. R. Foord, J.P., Mrs. Gibson, Mr. Jno. Gill (Royal Academy of Music), Mrs. Godfrey (Prince's Park, Liverpool), Mr. R. G. C. Hamilton, Mr. Vincent Hills, J.P., Mr. R. G. Hobbes, Miss Hogarth, Mr. Franklin Homan, Mr. John Jackson, Captain Henry James, R.N., Mr. S. Dyer Knott, Mr. A. Murphy, General Chas. Pasley, Mr. Pearce, Miss Grace Pearce, Mr. George Robinson, Mr. C. W. Sutton, Mr. S. Steele, J.P., Rev. H. B. Stevens, M.A., Mr. Chas. Roach Smith, F.S.A., Mr. Sketchly, Mr. Ald. John Tribe, Mr. Owen P. Thomas, Rev. Jno. Taylor, M.A., Mr. Humphrey Wickham, Mr. Wiggins, and in an especial manner to Mr. William Brenchley Rye, who has given me much valuable information which I could not otherwise have obtained.

Last, but not least, I wish to thank Mr. W. T. Wildish, of *The Rochester and Chatham Journal*, who, with a rare generosity, threw open the columns of his newspaper to assist me in my inquiries. My thanks to him must include several unknown correspondents of his and mine.

In conclusion, I may truly say that, from early associations of my own, and still more from a genuine admiration of the writings of Charles Dickens, this work has been to me a labour of love, for I recognise in Dickens a writer who, in his far-seeing humanity, has (more than any one in modern times, perhaps more than any one since Shakespeare) consecrated the English tongue to some of the highest purposes of which speech is capable.

ROBERT LANGTON.

CHAPTER I.

INTRODUCTORY.

" Every little incident, and even slight words and looks of those old days,——came fresh and thick before him many and many a time, and, rustling above the dusty growth of years, came back green boughs of yesterday."

Nicholas Nickleby, Part 2, Chap. XXXIII.

THE above paragraph is suggestive enough ; it was written in 1838, when the author was twenty-six years of age, and will serve for a theme for this and all the following chapters of this book. It is, besides, perhaps one of the earliest examples of the blank

B

verse to be found occasionally in the earlier writings of Charles Dickens.

It would be an easy matter to show that, in the past, nearly all our really great writers of fiction have left us, in their imaginative flights, more or less perfect sketches of their Autobiography ; and it is sometimes difficult (as indeed it should be) to determine where fiction terminates and fact begins.   This is perhaps more especially true of Charles Dickens than of any other writer.

I shall endeavour to show in the following brief narrative of his early years, how his own "childish imaginings" and experiences were, from the very first opening of his brilliant literary career, reproduced in his works.

This was apparent to many (though not to a full extent) long before Mr. Forster in his first volume of the life of his friend, astonished the reading world with his revelations in Chapter II., a chapter which has been somewhat heartlessly described by a contemporaneous writer as " The Blacking Bottle period."

Since these revelations were made it has become not only possible, but comparatively easy to trace the author's life in his books.

During the last few years, accordingly, we have had several attempts, both in England and America, to show how many of Dickens' characters, and incidents in his tales, are recollections of his own early experiences. These attempts, too, are (as indeed are most of the later criticisms of his works) all on one side—all friendly to the author.

In some of these essays, it is true, fiction is introduced, and in others the *facts* are funnier than the fiction ; as for instance where Portsea is said to be in Kent, and where we are told that Mr. Pickwick was imprisoned in Fleet Street! Others have apparently " wandered and lost their way " in a fruitless attempt to identify places that are past finding out, places indeed, which are intentionally and effectually beyond identification.[1]

So also, with many of the characters of Dickens. Not only have the works themselves a strong element of immortality about them, but this quality would seem to have descended upon some of the characters in his writings ; for if one could only believe all one is told, three separate and individual examples of " Bob Cratchit " are still in the flesh, all warranted to be indisputably the real Bob!

There are also still living two Sam Wellers, one of them described to me as " an aged man now "; and one

---

[1] Throughout the whole of the writings of Charles Dickens nothing is more noteworthy than the way in which many of the scenes of tales and incidents are only half revealed, or, as will be seen further on, purposely obscured or confused with other places.

each of Uriah Heep, Captain Cuttle, and Barnaby Rudge. The latter is farther reported to have been seen recently rushing through the streets of Rochester, his dilapidated dress by no means improved by the flight of time ! !

How far the fact that these and similar stories are believed by numbers of people all over England, should entitle them to some respect, I will not determine ; but I can answer for it that, save for the absolute impossibility of the existence of a dual "Sam" and a triple "Bob," other stories quite as remarkable and improbable have come to my knowledge, which stories have the additional attraction of being strictly true.

A single instance will suffice here. It is over fifty years since Mr. John Dickens (to be presently more particularly mentioned) left Mile-end Cottage, Alphington, near Exeter, and it is very nearly forty years since he departed this life. Yet, within the last few years, a letter was sent to him from America, to his old address. It was of course returned through the Dead Letter Office, and was most probably, says my informant (Mr. Rye), "a request from a Yankee collector for his autograph !"

It will be seen in the following chapters that much of my information is derived directly from aged persons of both sexes, who speak from their own personal recollections of Dickens when a boy. It is now twenty years since his death, and in that time many others of these old friends have departed to "the land where all things

HIGH STREET, ROCHESTER

are forgotten," and of those that remain "how few," as
Scott sings—

> " How few, all weak and withered of their force,
> Wait, on the verge of dark eternity."

It is greatly to be regretted that Mr. Forster did not,
twenty years ago, when writing the first volume of the life
of his friend, go thoroughly into these remembrances
of a noble boyhood, so much easier to be got at then
than now.

In the prosecution of my search for the new facts in
the early life of Dickens now first given to the world, I
was at one time somewhat staggered by the question—
" Do you suppose the family of an illustrious man like
Charles Dickens will thank you for raking up all these
details of his boyhood ? "

This query, coupled with the sentiments of Dickens
himself, expressed in a letter to Mr. William Sandys, dated
June 13th, 1847, required careful consideration. He says
(writing of Shakespeare), " It is a great comfort, to my
thinking, that so little is known concerning the poet. It
is a fine mystery, and I tremble every day lest something
should come out. If he had had a Boswell, society
wouldn't have respected his grave, but would calmly
have had his skull in the phrenological shop windows."

On mature reflection, however, it appeared to me
that, as I had found absolutely nothing in the early

childhood or surroundings of this great man that *any one* need be ashamed of, or that could give pain to relatives or friends, and that as the task would be certain to be attempted hereafter, when, for obvious reasons, much of this new matter would have been irrevocably lost, I could no longer hesitate.

I therefore send out this little book as another small contribution to the long list of works on Charles Dickens already before the public, a list that is growing longer every year, and in doing so earnestly hope that the narrative of these early days may interest many, and offend NOBODY!

FROM HOGARTH'S PEREGRINATIONS AT ROCHESTER AND ELSEWHERE.

CHAPTER II.

THE MARRIAGE OF JOHN DICKENS.

"And it is pleasant to write down that they reared a family; because any propagation of goodness and benevolence is no small addition to the aristocracy of nature, and no small subject of rejoicing for mankind at large."—*Old Curiosity Shop*, Chap. last.

"The chimes of the Church of St. Mary in the Strand."—*Uncommercial Traveller*.

OME genealogists tell us, and with perfect accuracy, that every man now living, whether Prince or Peasant, is sprung (only twenty generations back) from more than ONE MILLION FATHERS AND MOTHERS! The chief conclusion to be drawn from this very levelling fact (the truth of which may readily be proved by any one) is, that the whole world is kin, in a much more literal sense than is commonly supposed.

But not to go twenty generations back, nor five, how many comfortable, middle-class people, can tell even the surnames of their four Great Grandfathers ?

With a ready appreciation of this Vanity of Vanities, Dickens tells us, in the opening chapter of *Martin Chuzzlewit*, that "it may be laid down as a general principle that the more extended the ancestry, the greater the amount of violence and vagabondism."

Again, "The Chuzzlewits were connected by a bend sinister, or kind of Heraldic over the left, with some un-known noble and illustrious house." [Chap. I.] And looking at the matter from another side, in *Nicholas Nickleby* [Chap. VI.], he says, "a man who was born three or four hundred years ago, cannot reasonably be expected to have had so many relations before him, as a man who is born now."

Of the ancestry of Charles Dickens I can learn nothing. The only mention of a third generation in Mr. Forster's book is that in vol. i., page 42, where the little boy is said to have been possessed of "a fat old silver watch," which had been given him by his grandmother ; but whether paternal or maternal grandmother cannot probably now be known.

John Dickens, the father of Charles Dickens, was descended on both sides from well-to-do middle class parents, and that is all that is known, or can be said with certainty, of his pedigree.

He was born in 1786, probably in London, and is first traceable in the books of the Navy-Pay Office, at Somerset House, under date of 5th April, 1805, as seventh assistant clerk, with a salary of £80 per annum. He was then nineteen years of age; and four years afterwards, at the age of twenty-three, we can follow him across the street, to the beautiful church of St. Mary-le-Strand, where he was married to Elizabeth Barrow. The entry in the church register, and a *fac-simile* of the signatures of the principal contracting parties, is given below.

[The Year 1809.]   Page 5.

No. 17.   John Dickins of this Parish Bachelor and Elizabeth Barrow of this Parish, spinster a minor, were married in this church by licence by consent of her Father this Thirteenth day of June in the Year One Thousand Eight Hundred and Nine.   By me,

                                        J. J. Ellis, Curate.

This marriage was solemnised between us

John Dickens

Jo Elizabeth Barrow

In the presence of { Charles Barrow
                   { Mary Barrow   Sarah Barrow

And no doubt, though it be not written down, in the

presence of some of the junior clerks of the Navy-Pay, the more so as one of them, Mr. Thomas Barrow, was, by this ceremony, to become the brother-in-law of the bridegroom, Mr. John Dickens.

In the above entry, it is noticeable, first, that the curate has mis-spelt the name Dickens, for he has put a second *i* in the place of *e*; and secondly, John was evidently a little nervous, for he has commenced to write his name in the wrong place, the "Jo" remaining to this day to testify to the fact.

Immediately after their marriage (Mr. John Dickens having been "detached," as the phrase was in his department at that time, to attend the paying off of ships at Portsmouth) the young couple went to reside at Portsea, as is proved by Mr. Pearce's rent-book, the first quarter's rent (£8 15s.) having been paid September 29th, 1809. Here Fanny Dickens (Frances Elizabeth) was born, and the writer lately found the entry of her baptism in the register of St. Mary's, Portsea, under date November 23rd, 1810. Here they lived three years at the house shown in the engraving. It was in this house that our great humourist, Charles John Huffam Dickens (Charles after his maternal grandfather and John after his father) first saw the light. Another son, Alfred, who died in his infancy, was also born at Portsea.

CHAPTER III.

THE BIRTH OF CHARLES DICKENS.

"That boy, sir," said the Major, "will live in history. That boy, sir, is not a common production."

Dombey and Son, Chap. X.

"I WAS born (as I have been informed and believe) on a Friday, at twelve o'clock at night." Thus David Copperfield, and this is literally accurate of Charles Dickens, who was born at Portsea on Friday, the 7th February, 1812 (Leap Year), at a few minutes before midnight. When less than a month old, he was baptised at

St. Mary's, Kingston, the parish church of Portsea. The entry in the register is briefly thus [1] :—

BAPTISMS.

1812
March 4th { — Charles John Huff⁺ʰam S of John
    and   Elizabeth Dickens.

On the first page of Mr. Forster's *Life of Charles Dickens,* we find the entry of baptism as given above,

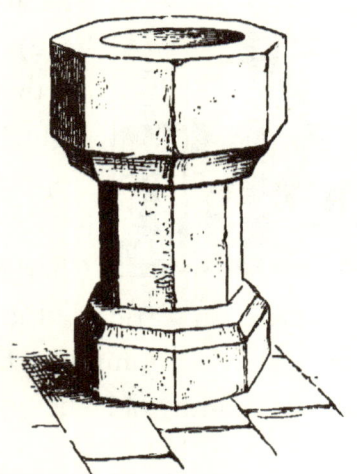

Old Font, St. Mary's, Portsea.

with the remark, " though on the very rare occasions when he subscribed that name, he wrote Huffam."

On this it is necessary to add that Huffam is

---

[1] The parish authorities at St. Mary's did not know they had the register of his baptism, till after his death, when the executors wrote for it.

THE HOUSE AT PORTSEA IN WHICH CHARLES DICKENS
WAS BORN.

undoubtedly the right spelling, and that the spelling in the register is an error. Besides bearing the name of his maternal grandfather, and father, as above-mentioned, the boy was named Huffam after his Godfather, Christopher Huffam," [1] described in the London Post Office Directory as " Rigger to His Majesty's Navy, Limehouse Hole."

The birthplace is No. 387, Commercial Road, Mileend, Landport, formerly known as Mile-end Terrace, and is so far in Portsea, as being in the island of that name. It is now occupied by Miss Grace Pearce, the daughter of the owner who was the landlord of Mr. John Dickens when Charles was born there.

Of the infancy of Charles Dickens at Portsea little can now be known ; it is, however, certain that in June quarter 1812 Mr. John Dickens left Mile-end Terrace and went to reside in Hawke Street, Portsea, the second house, in fact, past the boundary of Portsea. Captain Henry James, R.N., writes me (June 1885) : " The chief recollection I have of the family of Mr. Dickens was in 1812. They had left the house in which the great man was born, and I once saw the babe in long petticoats in their lodging in Portsea."

It is said that, in after years, Charles Dickens could remember places and things at Portsmouth that he had

---

[1] The name of Christopher occurs in three of Dickens' characters — Christopher Nubbles, Christopher Casby, and Christopher a waiter.

not seen since he was an infant of little more than two years old ; and there is no doubt whatever, that many of the earliest reminiscences of David Copperfield were also tender childish memories of his own infancy at this place.

For his sister Fanny mentioned above, it may be appropriately said here that Dickens evinced through life the tenderest attachment, and there are many unmistakable allusions to her in his works. In the *Haunted Man*, written in 1848, shortly after his sister's death, this passage occurs : " My sister, doubly dear, doubly devoted—lived on to see me famous,—and then died—died gentle as ever, happy, and with no concern but for her brother." Her name (Fanny) occurs as the names of characters in his books, and shorter tales, no less than eleven times ! In the *Experiences of a Barrister's Life*, by Serjeant Ballantine, vol. i., p. 138, the writer describes Fanny Dickens as "a young lady of great talents and accomplishments, who unfortunately died when still quite young." Again, in vol. ii., p. 137 (written January 10th, 1838), he says : " Evening party at Levien's. Met Boz—looks quite a boy. His sister was there ; she sang beautifully, is pretty, and I should think clever."

Fanny Dickens, afterwards Mrs. Burnett, died of consumption at the early age of thirty-eight.

Arms of Portsmouth.

Ordnance Terrace, Chatham.

CHAPTER IV.

ORDNANCE TERRACE, CHATHAM.

"My Boyhood's Home."—*Dullborough Town.*

"Second house in the Terrace."—*Ibid.*

IT is believed that Mr. John Dickens removed to Chatham in 1816, and Mr. Forster's account leans to this view, but if this be correct, it cannot now be settled where he lived for the first few months after his arrival at Chatham.

An exhaustive search in the Rate-books proves conclusively, however, that in 1817 (probably from Midsummer) Mr. Dickens was living at the house at first No. 2, but since altered to No. 11, Ordnance Terrace, Chatham. A view of the terrace is given on the opposite page, and the house is indicated by figures that will pass alike for 11 or 2, marked on the front.

Here he resided till Lady-Day, 1821, and in this house were born Harriet Ellen, in the autumn of 1819, and Frederick William in 1820. Both of these infants died in their childhood.

There are probably ten or twelve persons still living at Chatham or Rochester, who can remember his occupying this house, as also the house to be presently named, on the Brook.

It was during his residence here that some of the happiest years of the childhood of little Charles were passed, as his father was at this time in a fairly good position in the Navy-Pay Office, and was (without extras) from June 1815 to 1819 in receipt of £200 per annum, and in 1820 his salary was augmented to £350 per annum, at which latter sum it remained till he left the service, March 9th, 1825.

Mr. William Thomas Wright, for many years head of the Navy-Pay Office at Chatham Dockyard, remembered John Dickens at this time very well, and described him to my informant, Mr. W. B. Rye, formerly of the British Museum, late of Exeter, as " a fellow of infinite humour, chatty, lively, and agreeable ; and believed him capable to have imparted to his son Charles materials for some of the characteristic local sketches of men and manners, so graphically hit off in the early chapters of Pickwick."

He is described by another gentleman still living as being a thorough good fellow, and, speaking of the family

residing at Ordnance Terrace (at this time consisting of
Mr. and Mrs. Dickens, Fanny, Charles, Letitia, and
their maternal Aunt Mrs. Allen) he says, "they were a
most genial, loveable family," and no doubt "with something more than a ghost of gentility hovering in their
company."[1]

Ordnance Terrace is known to have furnished the
locality and characters for some of the early *Sketches by
Boz. The Old Lady* was a Mrs. Newnham who lived at
No. 5, which was then the last house in the Terrace, and
was, by all accounts, very kind to the Dickens children,
the youngest girl Letitia Mary, a very pretty child,
being her especial favourite. *The Half-Pay Captain*
was also a near neighbour of the Dickens family, and
was quite unconsciously sitting for his portrait to one
(a very little one) who was afterwards to immortalise
him in his earlier writings.

The next-door neighbours at No. 1, the corner house,
were the Stroughills, and George Stroughill the son,
somewhat older than Charles Dickens, was his greatest
friend during these happy years. Some characteristics
of George, a frank, open, and somewhat daring boy, are
reproduced as Steerforth in *David Copperfield*. His
sister Lucy, the Golden Lucy of *The Wreck of the Golden
Mary*, from her beautiful golden locks, was the especial
favourite and little sweetheart of Charles at this time.

[1] *Our French watering place.*

A quotation from *Sketches of Young Couples.—The old Couple* will fitly introduce here "an aged woman who once lived servant"—with the Dickens family,—"she nursed the children on her lap, and tended those who are no more—Death has not left her alone, and this with a roof above her head, and a warm hearth to sit by, makes her cheerful and contented,—she was as smart a young girl then as you'd wish to see." This old lady, still living in the neighbourhood, was in the service of the Dickens family both in Ordnance Terrace and in the house on the Brook.

Her vivid recollections of these far-off, happy days are "like the ghost of a departed time."[1] Her very suggestive maiden name was Mary Weller!!! She is now the wife of Mr. Thomas Gibson (formerly a shipwright in the Dockyard), to whom she has been married fifty-nine years!

This aged couple can both of them remember little Lucy,[2] the blue-eyed, golden-haired fairy, of whom little Charles (himself at this early age very fair) was the constant companion.

In Birthday Celebrations we come on a reminiscence of these early days which is unmistakable in this connection.

[1] *Our Mutual Friend*, vol. i., p. 311.
[2] The name Lucy occurs in five of the works of Dickens, as the Christian names of characters, and Lucie Manette in *A Tale of Two Cities*, is also said to have had golden hair!!

" I can very well remember being taken out to visit some peach-faced creature in a blue sash, and shoes to correspond, whose life I supposed to consist entirely of birthdays. Upon seed-cake, sweet wine, and shining presents, that glorified young person seemed to me to be exclusively reared. At so early a stage of my travels did I assist at the anniversary of her nativity (and became enamoured of her), that I had not yet acquired the recondite knowledge that a birthday is the common property of all who are born, but supposed it to be a special gift bestowed by the favouring heavens on that one distinguished infant. There was no other company, and we sat in a shady bower—under a table, as my better (or worse) knowledge leads me to believe—and were regaled with saccharine substances and liquids, until it was time to part."

["When will there come in after life a passion so earnest, generous, and true as theirs? What even in its gentlest realities can have the grace and charm that hover round such fairy lovers?"] *The Young Couple,* 1840.

Mrs. Gibson says : " Little Charles was a terrible boy to read, and his custom was to sit with his book in his left hand, holding his wrist with his right hand, and constantly moving it up and down, and at the same time sucking his tongue. Sometimes Charles would come downstairs and say to me, ' Now, Mary, clear the kitchen, we are going to have such a game,' and then George Stroughill would come in with his Magic Lantern, and they would sing, recite, and perform parts of plays.

Fanny and Charles often sang together at this time, Fanny accompanying on the pianoforte. Though a good and eager reader in these days (about 1819) he had certainly not been to school, but had been thoroughly well taught at home by his aunt and mother, and " (adds Mrs. Gibson, speaking of the latter) " she was a dear, good mother, and a fine woman."

" A rather favourite piece for recitation by Charles at this time was ' The Voice of the Sluggard ' from Dr. Watts, and the little boy used to give it with great effect, and with *such* action and *such attitudes*."

Readers will remember that Captain Cuttle introduces " the voice of the sluggard, announcing a quotation with his hook," also how in *Martin Chuzzlewit*, Chap. IX., Mr. Pecksniff, when urged to get to bed, makes a tipsy speech from the top landing of Mrs. Todger's, and treats his young friends to a full verse of this same "Moral Song."

Little Charles Dickens lives in Mrs. Gibson's memory as " a lively boy of a good, genial, open disposition, and not quarrelsome, as most children are at times."

In a note to Forster's *Life of Charles Dickens*, vol. i., p. 3, there is a portion of a letter dated Gad's Hill, 24th September, 1857, to this effect : " I feel much as I used to do when I was a small child a few miles off, and somebody (who I wonder, and which way did *She* go, when she died ?) hummed the Evening Hymn to me, and I cried on the pillow—either with the remorseful consciousness

THEATRE ROYAL, ROCHESTER.

of having kicked Somebody else, or because still Somebody else had hurt my feelings in the course of the day."

There is little reason to doubt that this singer of the Evening Hymn still survives in the person of Mrs. Gibson ;[1] for on asking her plainly without preparation, " Did you ever sing the Evening Hymn to the children ? " she replied, after a little reflection, " Yes, many a time," and seemed very much surprised by so unexpected a question.

Charles was now at from six to seven years of age in the fullest enjoyment of that happy period of life, when infancy is gradually giving place to boyhood, a period which he in later years remembered so tenderly, and described so well, " where everything was happy, where there was no distance and no time."[2]

{ From an early age he had been taken to the Theatre Royal at the foot of Star Hill, Rochester, and his experiences there will be found in another place. } The Theatre remains unaltered externally to the present day. It may be mentioned in passing that this theatre was built by a Mrs. Baker, whose daughter married the able and well-known actor Dowton, also that Edmund Kean, Charles Matthews, Joseph Grimaldi, and other great theatrical lights have in their time played many parts in this old house.

---

[1] Mrs. Mary Gibson died April 22nd, 1888, aged eighty-four years.
[2] *Martin Chuzzlewit*, Chap. LIII.

Charles was eight years of age and still living in " the Terrace," when he was taken to see Grimaldi, the celebrated clown, whose life he afterwards edited. " I was brought up from remote country parts in the dark ages of 1819 and 1820, to behold the splendour of Christmas Pantomime and the humour of Joe, in whose honour I am informed I clapped my hands with great precocity." Forster's *Life*, vol. i., p. 121.

It was chiefly during these halcyon days that Charles Dickens, being by this time stronger on his legs, made himself acquainted with the beauties of the surrounding country ; that he first saw Gad's Hill, the Falstaff, Chalk, and Cobham, Snorridge (Snowledge) bottom, Tom-all-alone's, and Frindsbury, and that he "peeped about the old corners" of the city of Rochester " with interest and wonder," imbibing as he delightedly did so that strong and enduring love for the locality, which was to last him thenceforward for the rest of his life ; when, fully fifty years afterwards in the neighbouring parish of Higham he too " went out with the tide." [1]

[1] *David Copperfield*, Chap. XXX.

THE MITRE INN, CHATHAM.

THE HOUSE ON THE BROOK, CHATHAM.

CHAPTER V.

THE MITRE.

"There was an inn in the Cathedral Town where I went to school, that had pleasanter recollections about it than any of these. . . . It had an ecclesiastical sign . . . The Mitre, . . . and a bar, that seemed to be the next best thing to a bishopric, it was so snug. I loved the landlord's youngest daughter to distraction,——but let that pass. It was in this inn that I was cried over by my rosy little sister,[1] because I had acquired a black eye in a fight. ' And though she had been, that holly-tree night, for many a long year where all tears are dried, the Mitre softened me yet."—*The Holly Tree*, 1858.

HE *Mitre Inn* and *Clarence Hotel* is noted in Wright's Guide to Rochester and Chatham (1838), as being "the Manor House, and a very old-established Hotel." An advertisement elsewhere in this guide states that "it is the first posting-house in the town."

[1] His sister Fanny died in 1848.

In 1820-21, a Mr. Tribe was the landlord and owner of this fine old house; and to this day it is the property, though not in the occupation, of his son, Mr. John Tribe, Alderman and ex-Mayor of Rochester.

At this old inn, about the close of the last century, Lord Nelson used to reside when on duty at Chatham, a room he occupied being known as " Nelson's Cabin " to this day. Here, too, King William the Fourth, when Duke of Clarence, used occasionally to stay, and hence the supplementary part of its sign, *The Clarence Hotel.*

The Mitre is now very much as it was when Charles Dickens knew it as a boy : its beautiful grounds remain as they were, a surprise and a delight to the stranger. " None of the old rooms were ever pulled down ; no old tree was ever rooted up ; nothing with which there was any association of byegone times was ever removed or changed." [1]

It was here (the families of Mr. Dickens and Mr. Tribe being on visiting terms) that little Charles used occasionally to sing, in a clear treble voice, some of those old songs which he was always fond of, and which he has since recalled many times in his writings. Sea-songs were at this time his especial favourites, and at a memorable party here, Mr. Tribe well remembers Charles and his sister Fanny mounted on a dining table for a stage,

[1] *Nicholas Nickleby*, Chap. XXXIII.

singing what was then a popular duet.   Here are the
first four stanzas (there are seven in all) :—

> Long time I've courted you, miss,
>   And now I'm come from sea ;
> We'll make no more ado, miss,
>   But quickly married be.
>   Sing fal de ral, etc.
>
> I ne'er will wed a tar, sir,
>   Deceitful as yourself ;
> 'Tis very plain you are, sir,
>   A good-for-nothing elf.
>   Sing fal de ral, etc.
>
> I ne'er deceived you yet, miss,
>   Though like a shrew you rave ;
> But prithee, scold and fret, miss,—
>   A storm I well can brave.
>   Sing fal de ral, etc.
>
> False man, you courted Sally,
>   You filled with vows her head ;
> And Susan in the valley,
>   You promised you would wed.
>   Sing fal de ral, etc.

The song ends, as of course it should, in mutual for-
bearance, and a complete reconciliation.

A most interesting relic of these Ordnance Terrace
and Mitre evenings, is still in the possession of Mr. Ald.
John Tribe.   It is a card of invitation written by Charles

when between eight and nine years of age. Unfortunately the card itself, an address card of his father's, has been temporarily mislaid, or it would have been reproduced here in *fac-simile*, as the earliest piece of writing of Charles Dickens known to be in existence. Mr. Tribe can, however, remember it is to this effect.[1]

Master and Miss Dickens will be pleased to have the company of Master and Miss Tribe to spend the Evening on . . . [date, etc.]

At birthday parties, Twelfth night parties, and ordinary evening parties, at the Mitre, at Ordnance Terrace, and elsewhere, and in juvenile picnics in the hayfield in front of the terrace (now swallowed up by the Chatham Railway Station), the accomplishments of Charles and his sister were often utilised to amuse the company.

The mention of the comic singing to his friend, Mr. Forster, many long years afterwards, was accompanied with a modestly expressed fear that " he must have been

---

[1] Mr. Ald. John Tribe is since dead.

The Old Pay-Office Yacht (Chatham).

View of Rochester from Chatham.
(*After* Dadson.)

a horrible little nuisance to many unoffending grown-up people who were called upon to admire him." The evidence is, however, all the other way, and Mr. Tribe, Mrs. Gibson, Mrs. Godfrey (a sister of Mr. William Giles, his schoolmaster), and others, can remember perfectly that these songs were warmly applauded by all, and justly so, for they were admirably sung.

Many of these old ditties are, however, aptly described in *Great Expectations*, thus : " I thought (as I still do) the amount of Too-ral somewhat in excess of the poetry." Chap. XV.

For very many years both before and after this time, there was stationed at Chatham an old-fashioned, high-sterned sailing-yacht, pierced with circular ports, and dating from the time of the Commonwealth. She was called the *Chatham*, and was indifferently known as the Commissioners' Yacht, or the Navy-Pay Yacht. In this vessel Charles and his sisters were sometimes taken for a sail on the Medway by their father, when he went to Sheerness, on the business of the Pay Office. " It was a grand treat," says one who has himself enjoyed it, " but it was expressly stipulated that great order and decorum should be observed on board."

The accompanying engraving of this yacht is from Milton's large Plan of Chatham Dockyard in 1755. With a light wind she was a sluggish sailer, but in a

---

[1] Mr. W. B. Rye.

stiff breeze, she sometimes fairly astonished the blue-jackets engaged in sailing her, by her great speed and general handiness.

The old craft was, after a career extending over considerably more than two centuries, finally broken up at Chatham in 1868.

While living in Ordnance Terrace the name of John Dickens frequently occurs in local subscription lists raised for a variety of purposes ; it appears, for instance, in the printed list of subscribers to Wildash's *History of Rochester*, published in 1817. In 1820 (March 3rd) a calamitous fire occurred in Chatham, by which thirty-eight houses were consumed, and many families rendered houseless and desolate. A relief committee was immediately formed, and of this Mr. John Dickens was an active and conspicuous member, and a subscriber of two guineas to the fund. In his report, printed in 1821, the treasurer, Mr. W. Jefferys, returned thanks for the efficient and valuable services rendered by Mr. Dickens at that time.

It will perhaps interest readers to know that the second or supplementary account of this fire, in the *Times* of the 4th March, 1820, was written by Mr. John Dickens !

" But, alas ! these high and palmy days had taken to themselves boots, and were already walking off." [1] The

---

[1] *Nicholas Nickleby,* Chap VI.

money involvements of Mr. Dickens, and consequent necessary retrenchment mentioned by Mr. Forster as being first noticeable in London on his recall from Chatham, were really in existence in 1821. The cause of his difficulties can be traced with certainty ; he was by all obtainable accounts an open-handed, most generous, and easy-going man, and this is doing him but the barest justice.

On the other hand he is known to have been somewhat too lavish in his expenditure, and in short, in the language of the immortal Sam, " He run a match agin the constable and van it."[1]

[1] *Pickwick*, Chap. XLI.

CHAPTER VI.

THE HOUSE ON THE BROOK.

"The home of his infancy—to which his heart had yearned with an intensity of affection not to be described."

Pickwick, Chap. VI.

"This has been a Happy Home, John!"

Cricket on the Hearth.

THE account given by Mr. Forster of the residence of Mr. John Dickens, at Chatham, on page 3 of vol. i. of the *Life*, is that it was "in St Mary's Place, otherwise called the Brook, and next door to a Baptist meeting-house called Providence Chapel, of which a Mr. Giles, to be presently mentioned, was minister. Charles at this time was between four and five years old; and here he stayed till he was nine."

That the biographer of Dickens should have omitted all mention of the house in Ordnance Terrace, where, as has been shown, his friend lived for four pregnant years of his youthful life, is a curious fact ; it is also an instance of his frequent inaccuracy as to these early days !

Charles was beyond all question over nine years of age when he left Ordnance Terrace, and his father occupied the smaller house on the Brook for fully a year and a half, as will be shown farther on. It will therefore be evident that, instead of Charles Dickens being nine years old when he left Chatham, as stated by Forster, he must have been nearly if not quite eleven. His own account in a letter to Mr. Wilkie Collins, June 6th, 1856, is, " I was taken to Chatham when I was very young, and lived and was educated there till I was twelve or thirteen, I suppose." Of this, however, more will be said in its place.

It was early in the year 1821 that for reasons already indicated, Mr. Dickens removed from No. 2 in Ordnance Terrace, and took up his abode in a much smaller house on the Brook, originally so named from a stream of water (now covered over) that comes down from the higher grounds, and falls into the Medway.

The house itself, No. 18, St. Mary's Place, is absolutely unaltered in the sixty years that have elapsed since John Dickens and his young and growing family lived there ;

it must, however, be admitted that time has made a sad change for the worse in the character of this neighbourhood. The engraving will enable the reader to identify the house; it is the one next door to the little Baptist Chapel (now the Salvation Drill Hall!) where the Rev. William Giles, father of Mr. Giles, the schoolmaster at this time, officiated.

While Mr. Dickens lived here, Mary Weller again took service in his family, and she (Mrs. Gibson) sorrowfully remembers the altered circumstances under which they now lived. "There were," she says, "no such juvenile entertainments at this house as I had seen at the Terrace."

The house on the Brook is near St. Mary's, the Parish Church of Chatham, where three children of John and Elizabeth Dickens, viz., Harriett Ellen (September 3rd, 1819), and Frederick William (August 4th, 1820), born at Ordnance Terrace, and another son to be presently mentioned, were baptized. A view of this church from a lithograph of the time by Mr. William Dadson, drawing-master of Rochester, is given here, as is also a view of Rochester from near the Sun Pier, Chatham, by the same artist. The latter engraving illustrates an effect Dickens was very fond of, and which he uses repeatedly in his works, that of a long path of light either from the moon, as in *David Copperfield*,[1] or from the setting sun reflected on the water.

ST. MARY'S CHURCH, CHATHAM.
(*After* W. DAWSON.)

THE NAVY-PAY OFFICE, CHATHAM DOCKYARD.

This engraving also shows the distant cathedral with a *spire*,[1] as it was till the year 1825, when the church restorers of those days took it down and altered the tower as we see it now.

From an upper window in the side of this house in St. Mary's Place, the parish church and churchyard can be seen, exactly as described in *A Child's Dream of a Star*, written in 1850. This little tale is a very touching reminiscence of his own and his sister's childhood here.

The new residence was also much nearer to the dockyard, and Charles, who "strolled about a good deal, and thought of a number of things"[2] now formed an accurate and lasting idea of the "Yard."

Near the handsome substantially built row of houses where the leading officials of the yard reside, stands the Navy-Pay Office, an old-fashioned, red brick pile, with heavily barred windows, and strong rooms lined throughout with iron. Through the courtesy of the Admiral Superintendent, I am enabled to give here a sketch of this unpretending eminently practical looking building.

It was here, in the room lately occupied by the

[1] "I remember how I seemed to float, then down the melancholy glory of that track upon the sea, away into the world of dreams."— *David Copperfield*, Chap. XIII. See also *American Notes*, Chaps. XV. and XVI.

[2] *The Child's Dream of a Star.*

cashier, Mr. R. G. Hobbes, that Mr. John Dickens attended to his duties for six years, and here Charles came with him many a time. The building both externally and internally is, at the present day, exactly as it was during Dickens' childhood at Chatham.

In *The Uncommercial Traveller*, we are told of Chatham Dockyard, that "There is a gravity upon its red brick offices and houses, a staid pretence of having nothing worth mentioning to do, an avoidance of display, which I never saw out of England."

Here, as a boy, Dickens was never tired of watching the rope-makers, the anchor-smiths (nine of them at once, like "the muses in a ring"), and the block-makers at their work, and he seems to have taken more than a childish interest in the gradual development of the huge "wooden walls" on the slips.

In his boyhood a custom prevailed at Chatham Dockyard, for the blacksmiths to get up a pageant in honour of their patron saint, on St. Clement's Day, the 23rd November. The procession was usually headed by a band, and "Old Clem."[1] was enacted by a sturdy young smith, disguised for the occasion in a mask and flowing wig, and sitting in a chair of state. Speeches were made, doggrel rhymes recited, and black mail collected on their way through the town.

---

[1] "Old Clem." was, of course, merely a familiar term of endearment for St. Clement.

In *Great Expectations*, written in 1860, we find a distinct allusion to this custom in a song sung by Joe Gargery, Old Orlick, and Pip ; it occurs several times in the tale, and readers will probably remember the refrain " Beat it out, beat it out,—Old Clem ! with a clink for the stout—Old Clem ! "

These were the days when mechanics, fitters, and rivetters had not in a great measure taken the place of shipwrights. He tells us in his *Nurse's Stories* that " nails and copper are shipwrights' sweethearts, and ship-wrights will run away with them whenever they can." This, however, is almost a thing of the past, not so much because wooden ships are now partially superseded by ironclads, nor that copper nails and bolts are less used than formerly, but because the copper being " portable property " is better looked after, and also, let us hope, because there is an improvement in the men them-selves.

A change, too, has come over this yard in many ways. In the first place it is incomparably larger than before, and a novel feature is the introduction of loco-motive engines for carrying the heavy iron-work used for shipbuilding. Instead of this, in Dickens' early days and long since then, long files of convict labourers, guarded by soldiers, might be seen carrying planks of oak, the tall men bearing all the weight, and the little men walking in their places with their shoulders two or

E

three inches below the plank, and contentedly carrying nothing !

But although to some extent the very air of the place, once redolent of oak chips and shavings, of oakum, tarred ropes, and canvas, has changed ; yet, on the

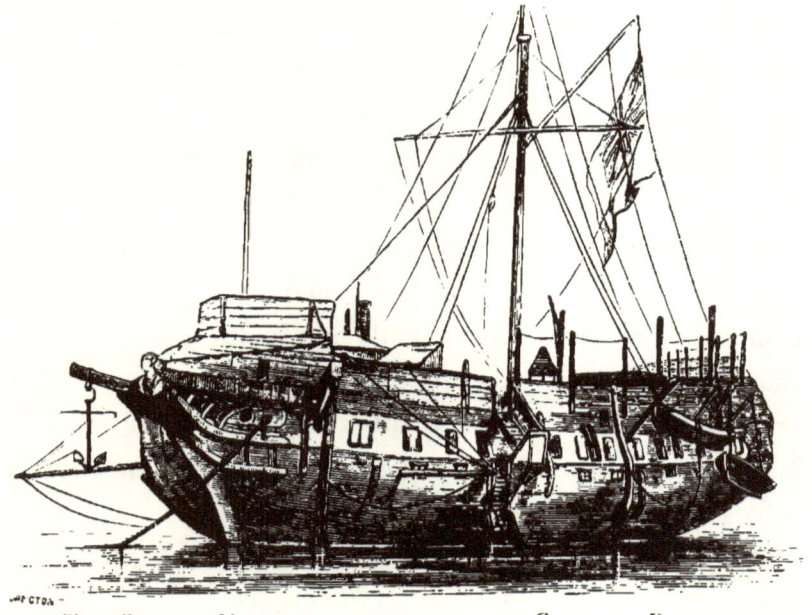

THE CONVICT HULK, FORMERLY LYING OFF CHATHAM DOCKYARD.

whole, the appearance of the older part of the yard is much the same now as when Charles Dickens was a boy there.

Lying off the dockyard at this time was the "receiving ship" (see illustration), one of the hulks to which the convicts "with great numbers on their backs

as if they were street doors,"[1] returned after their labour
in the dockyard, every man being searched before he
went on board for the night. To this particular hulk all
the fresh arrivals from London were drafted, and these
were the " ships roofed like Noah's Arks," that the little
boy would, no doubt, take an absorbing interest in.

" And please, what's Hulks ? " inquires little Pip, and
his sister replies : " Hulks are prison ships right 'cross
the meshes (marshes). People are put in the Hulks
because they murder, and because they rob, and forge,
and do all sorts of bad ; and they always begin by
asking questions." *Great Expectations*, Chap. II.

There are in this tale many allusions to convict life
at Chatham, and among them an account of how in the
old coaching days convicts were removed from London ;
and how passengers on the box seat were disagreeably
made aware of their presence, by feeling their breath on
the back of their necks, and by their " bringing with
them that curious flavour of bread-poultice, baize, rope-
yarn, and hearthstone, which attends the convict
presence " (Chap. XXVIII.).

During their residence on the Brook, a wedding took
place in the Dickens family, which it may be well to
mention with some fulness here ; perhaps the better way
to introduce it, will be to give the entry from the Church
Register.

[1] *Great Expectations*, Chap. XXVIII.

Page 101.

Marriages solemnized in the Parish of Chatham, in the County of Kent, in the year 1821.

Matthew Lamert of this Parish, Surgeon, Widower, and Mary Allen of this Parish, Widow were married in this Church by licence this eleventh day of December in the year one thousand eight hundred and twenty one.

By me W. H. Drage Curate.

This marriage was solemnized { Matthew Lamert
between us { Mary Allen

In the presence of { Elizabeth Dickens
{ John Dickens

George Elliott
Jno. H. Barrow.

No. 302

At the wedding of their aunt " Fanny " (called so by the children, though her name was Mary), Charles and his sister were also present, and on the departure of the married couple, James Lamert came to live with the family for the first time. Jane Bonny, a fellow-servant with Mary Weller, at Ordnance Terrace, went to Ireland with Mrs. Lamert, as her servant, and was with her when she died there, soon afterwards. It will be remembered that the rather remarkable name of this old servant occurs as the name of one of the characters in *Nicholas Nickleby*.

The above James Lamert, mentioned also in Mr. Forster's *Life of Dickens*, vol. i., page 11, as "a sort of cousin by marriage," was simply Dr. Lamert's son by his former wife. Mrs. Allen was *not* his step-mother; Mrs. Lamert undoubtedly was.

James Lamert was considerably older than his cousin Charles, but was, no doubt, attracted by a certain precocious smartness and intelligence in the little fellow's appearance and manner, qualities which endeared him at once to all who became acquainted with him, and which are remembered to this day by a few of his contemporaries still surviving at Chatham and Rochester.

Young Lamert not only took Charles to the theatre at Rochester, but himself got up some private theatricals in the spacious buildings of the Ordnance Hospital, not far from the dockyard, and his father, Dr. Lamert, sometimes took a part in these performances. Dr. Lamert and Dr. Slammer (of *Pickwick*) are of course the same person.

The regimental surgeon's kindly manner, and his short, odd ways of expressing himself, still survive in the recollections of a few old people.

CHAPTER VII.

GILES'S SCHOOL.

"It (the school) was very gravely and decorously ordered, and on a sound system; with an appeal in everything, to the honour and good faith of the boys, and an avowed intention to rely on their possession of those qualities, unless they proved themselves unworthy of it, which worked wonders."

David Copperfield, Chap. XVI.

IT is the opinion of persons who can in their own memories bridge over the gulf of more than sixty years, that Charles Dickens never went to a regular school till about Lady-Day, 1821. A preparatory school in Rome Lane (now Railway Street) is confidently mentioned by Mr. Forster, and it may be that for a short time he did attend such a school, but there is no obtainable evidence of the fact now.

It seems to me that the biographer of Dickens has gone a little out of his way to cast a slur upon the parents of his friend, when he says on page 6 of his first volume, " It will not appear, as my narrative moves on, that he owed much to his parents," because what follows would seem to falsify that statement ; " but he (Charles Dickens) has frequently been heard to say that his first desire for knowledge, and his earliest passion for reading, were awakened by his mother, who taught him the first rudiments not only of English, but also, a little later, of Latin. She taught him every day for a long time, and taught him, he was convinced, thoroughly well.".

His description of himself to Washington Irving, as " a small and not-over-particularly-taken-care-of boy," cannot fairly be said to apply to this early, happy period of his life.

It was during the residence at Ordnance Terrace that the mother and aunt educated the children at home, and on moving to the Brook, Charles and his sister Fanny were at once sent to Mr. Giles's school.

Some confusion has arisen as to which of the three houses in which Mr. Giles resided at Chatham was the school of Charles Dickens, but the evidence, that of Mr. Dickeson and others, who went to this school, is at once clear and beyond question.

Mr. William Giles, the son of the Rev. William Giles, the minister of Providence Chapel on the Brook, commenced school-keeping at a house in Clover Lane, now Clover Street, Chatham, and at that time his scholars consisted of his own younger brothers and sisters, of the children of some of the officers of the garrison, and a few of the children of the neighbours.

He shortly afterwards moved to the large house still standing at the corner of Rhode Street and Best Street shown in the initial letter of this chapter, and closely adjoining Clover Lane, and here Charles and Fanny Dickens attended as scholars. Finally he moved to Gibraltar Place on the new road. The school still lives in the memory of numbers of people resident in these towns (Strood, Rochester, Chatham, and Brompton), and a doggerel survives which runs thus :—

> Baker's Bull Dogs,
> Giles's Cats,
> New-road scrubbers,
> Troy Town Rats.

And in this rhyme four of the principal educational establishments of sixty years ago (in these towns) are named.

Mr. Giles had been educated at Oxford, was an accomplished scholar, and a very conscientious, pains-taking man. He seems to have been much struck (could not fail to have been so) with the bright appearance and unusual intelligence of his little pupil, and, giving him every encouragement in his power, even to making a companion of him of an evening, he was soon rewarded by the marked improvement that followed. Charles made rapid progress, and there is no doubt whatever that his wonderful knowledge and felicitous use of the English language in after life was, in a great measure, due to the careful training of Mr. Giles, who was widely known as a cultivated reader and elocutionist.

Mrs. Godfrey, the eldest sister of Mr. Giles, a venerable lady, now (1882) in her eighty-ninth year, residing at Liverpool, has kindly given me her recollections of Charles Dickens as a school-boy. She was some fifteen or sixteen years older than Charles, and was, consequently, well able to form an opinion of the appearance, manners, and capabilities of her brother's little pupil. Her recollection of him is, that he was a very handsome boy, with long curly hair of a light colour, and that he was of a very amiable, agreeable disposition. He was capital company even then (at nine or ten years of age), and she saw a great deal of him.

She clearly remembers both the house at Ordnance Terrace, and that on the Brook ; she also recognised the drawing of Providence Chapel as her father's chapel. She remembered the Mitre Inn very well—had dined there, and had a vivid recollection of the grounds at the back. She can remember that "Charles was quite at home at all sorts of parties, junketings, and birthday celebrations, and that he took great delight in Fifth of November festivities round the bonfire."

Mrs. Godfrey denies with some warmth the statement of Mr. Forster, that her brother taught his old pupil the bad habit of taking snuff, even "in very moderate quantities." She holds that the presentation of a silver snuffbox does not necessarily bind the recipient to any such habit.

At Mr. Giles's school the boys were expected to wear (and did wear) white beaver hats ; Charles Dickens was wearing such a hat when he left Chatham, and it will be remembered that in Forster's *Life*, vol. i., page 42, Charles went, during his father's difficulties, to the official appraiser, in order that his clothes might be inspected,— "certainly, the hardest creditor would not have been disposed to avail himself of my poor white hat," etc. So also in *David Copperfield*, Chap. X. : "Behold me on the morrow in a much worn little white hat ; " see also the late Mr. Hablot K. Browne's etching, where David appears before his aunt, Miss Betsey Trotwood, at Dover, in a much-battered white hat.

Notwithstanding the trouble and difficulties that had come upon the family, the children were happy enough at this time. There was—as Hood quaintly says—"sky-blue in their cup," they had many a romp in the Fort

Pitt Fields with Mary Weller, and the young shipwright, her sweetheart, "they were not always learning ; they had the merriest games that ever were played. They rowed upon the river in summer, and skated upon the ice in winter.—They had holidays, too, and Twelfth cakes, and parties, where they danced till midnight.—As to friends, they had such dear friends, and so many of them, that I want time to reckon them up. They were all young, like the handsome boy." [1]

Then the theatrical entertainments were still kept up, all through the closing months of 1821, and the spring of 1822. In the autumn of the former year he had distinguished himself by writing a tragedy called *Misnar*, the Sultan of India, and his singing, and recitation of humorous pieces was still much admired.

Charles was much beloved by his juvenile friends at school, and he was as full of fun (and it must be added of mischief) as any of them. The "lingo" said to have been invented by Dickens at a later period of school experiences in London, undoubtedly dated from this time, and was well known here.

In the summer and autumn he was frequently at Tom-all-alone's with his schoolfellows and friends, and witnessed the sham fights and siege operations, which at that time were carried on there as well as on "Chatham Lines." It will be remembered that in *Bleak House*

---

[1] *The Child's Story*, 1852

Tom-all-alone's is thus mentioned : " Twice, lately, there has been a crash and a cloud of dust, like the springing of a mine, in Tom-all-alone's, and, each time, a house has fallen."

Mr. Hobbes, the late cashier of Chatham Dockyard, has kindly furnished me with the following account of the origin of the curious name given to this place. " About 1747 one Thomas Clark, living at what is now called ' Old Brompton,' in order to break away from companions of whom he desired to get quit, bought a piece of waste ground some half-mile from the town, and built himself a house there. There he lived about twenty-five years *by himself*, and when returning home of an evening used to go crying or singing ' Tom's all alone !' Hence the place became known as ' Tom-all-alone's.' Tom by-and-by married, and had a large family ; and, as the children grew up, they married, and had large families too, and together they formed a little distinct colony. The Convict Prison, however, was to be built ; the ground on which ' Tom-all-alone's ' stood was wanted, and it was taken, and now belongs to the Prison."

There can be no doubt that the above passage from *Bleak House* was a reminiscence of the springing of a veritable mine he had witnessed at Tom-all-alone's, and that the name of the rookery where poor " Jo " lived in London, is taken from that locality. His playful description of the origin of the name in Chapter XVI. has an additional meaning now the site is turned into a Convict Prison ; " or, whether the traditional title is a comprehensive name for a retreat cut off from honest company, and put out of the pale of hope, perhaps nobody knows."

During these school-days at Chatham, Charles had, we are glad to know, access to his father's books, which, by a happy coincidence, numbered among them some of the best works of fiction to be found in our language,— those of Defoe, Smollett, Goldsmith, Fielding, and others ; also *The Spectator, The Tatler, The Idler, The Citizen of the World,* and *Mrs. Inchbald's Collection of Farces.* These were studied over and over again, and the world is probably the richer for his eager boyish perusal of them !

It will interest the reader to know that several of the incidents and names of characters contained in these famous works have been skilfully utilised by Dickens. They will be more fully referred to in their proper places in the Retrospective notes.

David Copperfield mentions these books as being in " a little room upstairs to which I had access (for it adjoined my own), and which nobody else in our house ever troubled." Had David's *alter ego* this room in his mind when in 1859 he wrote his Christmas story of *The Haunted House ?* In *The Ghost in Master B.'s Room,* in that tale he says, " Ah, me ; ah, me ! no other ghost has haunted the boys' room, my friends, since I have occupied it, than the ghost of my own childhood, the ghost of my own innocence, the ghost of my own airy belief."

That Dickens should in after life have manifested a love for all things nautical, that he should himself have looked at times like a sailor, and that the warmest sympathies of a naturally warm heart were always at the service of naval and merchant seamen, fishermen, Deal boatmen, and " great sea-porkypines " generally, where is the wonder ?

Was he not born within hearing of " the great voice of the sea, with its eternal nevermore " ? [1] Was he not the son, the grandson, and the godson of men directly connected with shipping and the sea ? Finally, was he not till eleven years of age brought up at a great Naval Depôt ?

That his age was really eleven and not nine, as has been stated when he left Chatham, I shall now endeavour to show. The family of Mr. John Dickens were all this time, while Charles was at Giles's School, still living on the Brook. We have seen that they were living there at the time of the marriage of Mrs. Allen to Dr. Lamert, in December 1821. They were living there when, in the spring of 1822 (March 11th), another son was born, and

---

[1] *David Copperfield,* Chap. XLVI.

here is a copy of the register of his baptism at St. Mary's Church.

April 3rd, 1822.—Alfred Lamert, Son of John and Elizabeth Dickens, Navy-Pay Office, Chatham.[1]

Mr. Dickens and his family continued to reside here, it is believed, all through this year, though no record of the date of his recall exists in the books at Somerset House ; and they left for London, according to such evidence as can be obtained, in the winter of 1822 and 1823, taking with them as a "small servant a girl from Chatham Workhouse." Her name cannot now be traced, as the books of that date are no longer in existence. The family left Chatham by coach, and their heavy goods were sent by water.[2]

Mrs. Godfrey believes that when the Dickens family finally left Chatham, Charles was (almost at the last minute) left with her brother Mr. Giles, with whom he remained for some little time longer ; and this would appear to be corroborated by his own account of the journey in the next chapter.

[1] He died in Manchester, July 1860.

[2] Mr. Gibson, who married Mary Weller, purchased Mr. John Dickens' parlour chairs on his leaving Chatham for London.

CHAPTER VIII.

LEAVES CHATHAM FOR LONDON.

"The light mists were solemnly rising, as if to show me the world, and I had been so innocent and little there, and all beyond was so unknown and great."

Great Expectations, Chap. XIX.

GOING AWAY, sadly enough, from all that had "given his ailing little life its picturesqueness or sunshine.' This must be the burden of the present chapter!

It is most probable that Charles Dickens left Chatham in the early months of 1823. His own account in *Dullborough Town* (1860) is as follows: "As I left Dullborough in the days when there were no railroads in the land, I left it in a stage-coach. Through all the years that have since passed have I ever lost the smell of the damp straw in which I was packed—like game—and forwarded, carriage paid, to the Cross Keys, Wood Street, Cheapside, London? There was no other inside passenger, and I consumed my sandwiches in solitude and dreariness, and it rained hard all the way, and I thought life sloppier than I had expected to find it. The coach that carried me away was melodiously called Timpson's Blue-eyed Maid, and belonged to Timpson, at the coach office up street."

This unmistakable reminiscence of his own journey to London, where he describes himself as being the only inside passenger, appears to confirm Mrs. Godfrey's account of the detention of Charles at Chatham, at his good schoolmaster's, till the family could get settled in a new home. It may be mentioned that Timpson was (with the alteration of a single letter) Simpson the coach proprietor, and that *The Blue-eyed Maid*[1] was a veritable coach, which as it started from Brompton would be more convenient for the Dickens family when resident on the Brook than the *Commodore* mentioned by Mr. Forster.

From some reminiscences of Rochester by the Rev. Walter A. Vaughan, his friend Mr. W. B. Rye has kindly sent me the following note : " The Commodore Coach

[1] The Blue-eyed Maid is also mentioned in *Little Dorrit*, Chap. III.

F

was driven by old Cholmeley (or Chumley), who was entrusted with all young ladies going to town. He made that celebrated speech about coaches when railways came in, 'If a railway blows up—where are ye? Now if a coach upsets *there* ye are!' I believe that originally came from him." Mr. Rye adds, "Old Chumley was a *character*, and was a first-rate whip; some amusing anecdotes of him are told in *Nimrod's Northern Tour*."

It would seem that shortly after the return of the Dickens family to London, one of the younger children born at Ordnance Terrace had died, and Charles was sent home to the funeral. The following quotation from one of the Christmas Stories, *The Haunted House*, is too probably a literal description of what now occurred.

" I was taken home, and there was Debt at home as well as Death, and we had a sale there. My own little bed was so superciliously looked upon by a power unknown to me, hazily called 'The Trade,' that a brass coal-scuttle, a roasting-jack, and a bird-cage, were obliged to be put into it to make a Lot of it, and then it went for a song,—so I heard mentioned, and I wondered what song,—and thought what a dismal song it must have been to sing."

The whole story of this sad period of the boy's life is indeed a dismal song to sing, and the only satisfaction to be derived from a perusal of Mr. Forster's painful account is, that good did really come out of his hard experiences at last ; for not only have we his humorous and comprehensive sketches of struggling, hopeless poverty in London and elsewhere, but he has left us that which will live still longer,—his kindly, pathetic tribute to the good qualities often to be found amongst those who are in necessity and tribulation.

On the arrival of Charles in London, in the spring of 1823, he entered at once upon a new life, and had to face a world of uncongenial surroundings abroad, and an ever increasing poverty at home. He now lived (for a few months only) at Camden Town, and whilst there his sister Fanny was admitted as a pupil at the Royal Academy of Music, then recently established. My note from the books of the Academy shows the date of entry : " Frances Elizabeth, daughter of John Dickens, Clerk in the Navy-Pay Office, of 16, Bayham Street, Camden Town, entered for the Piano. Admitted April 9th, 1823. Recommended and nominated by Thomas Tomkisson, Esq.[1] Left at Midsummer, 1827."

The family soon after left Bayham Street, and went to reside in a house in Gower Street, with a view, we are told, of Mrs. Dickens trying what she could do to help their resources by keeping a school. It was thought, says Mr. Forster, that the godfather, the rigger and block maker at Limehouse Hole, might introduce pupils, as he

---

[1] This Mr. Tomkisson was a Pianoforte Maker, of 77, Dean Street, Soho.

was a man of some influence and position, and had an Indian connection.

It was trusting to a broken reed, for he too succumbed to the general mercantile depression of the disastrous years 1823 and 1824, and was made a bankrupt, about the same time that Mr. John Dickens' misfortunes culminated in his arrest.

"Poor Mrs. Micawber! She said she had tried to exert herself; and so, I have no doubt, she had. The centre of the street door was perfectly covered with a great brass plate, on which was engraved: 'Mrs. Micawber's Boarding Establishment for Young Ladies;' but I never found that any young ladies had ever been to school there; or that any young lady ever came, or proposed to come; or that the least preparation was ever made to receive any young lady." [1]

With the alteration of the name only, this, says Forster, accurately describes this futile attempt to open a school. There is another distinct and humorous reference to these times in *Our Mutual Friend*, Chap. IV.

"'Yes,' said Mrs. Wilfer, 'the man came himself with a pair of pincers, and took it off, and took it away. He said that as he had no expectation of ever being paid for it, and as he had an order for another Ladies' School door-plate, it was better (burnished up) for the interests of all parties.'"

[1] *David Copperfield*, Chap. XI.

At length, all attempts to conciliate hostile creditors, or to get farther time, having failed, the father of the family was arrested, and conveyed to one of the debtors' prisons on the Surrey side of the Thames. There is some doubt or confusion as to which, and it arises thus : Mr. Forster makes the strange mistake of saying, on page 23 of his first volume of the *Life*, " The readers of Mr. Micawber's history, who remember David's first visit to the *Marshalsea* Prison,"—when we are distinctly told in the seventh chapter of *David Copperfield*, " At last, Mr. Micawber's difficulties came to a crisis, and he was arrested early one morning, and carried over to the *King's Bench* prison, in the Borough. He told me as he went out of the house, that the God of day had now gone down upon him, and—I really thought his heart was broken, and mine too."

Also in Chapter XLIX., in a letter, Mr. Micawber makes an appointment to meet David and Traddles at this spot, "among other havens of domestic tranquillity and peace of mind, my feet will naturally tend towards the King's Bench Prison. In stating that I shall be (D.V.) on the outside of the south wall of that place of incarceration on civil process, the day after to-morrow, at seven in the evening, precisely, my object in this epistolary communication is accomplished." And, says David, on getting to the place, "we found Mr. Micawber already there. He was standing with his arms folded, over against the wall, looking at the spikes on the top, with a sentimental expression, as if they were the interlacing boughs of trees that had shaded him in his youth."

For this and other reasons it seems probable that Mr. Dickens was confined in the King's Bench, and here is a rather singular and suggestive fact, which would seem to confirm that view. During the time Mr. John Dickens is known to have been in *a* debtor's prison (1824), a Mr. Dorrett (of Rochester too) was a prisoner for debt in the King's Bench! This is, perhaps, beyond question, as it is from the *London Gazette* of that date!

Mention is made of the King's Bench Prison in *Nicholas Nickleby*, Chap. XLVI., where Walter Bray[1] is said to have lived within the rules of the King's Bench, in *David Copperfield*, quoted above, and in the *Uncommercial Traveller* (night walks), where in a few powerful lines the author traces the progress of Dry-Rot in men, and tells how it "carried Horace Kinch inside the wall of the old King's Bench Prison, and it had carried him out with his feet foremost."

Mention is also made of the Marshalsea in *Pickwick* as the prison where George Heyling was incarcerated, and in *Little Dorrit* the first half of the book centres in the Marshalsea.

Of his description of the Fleet Prison, and of the

[1] Richard Bray was an old schoolfellow at Wellington House Academy.

monstrous cruelty and injustice practised there, and in all such . places, the readers of the works of Charles Dickens will be quite familiar ; scarcely three-score years have elapsed since these hard experiences overtook his family, but it has sufficed, and all these vile dens, with their accompanying retinue of sponging-house keepers, tipstaffs, and bailiffs, have passed away, and it is certain that, in the near future, their very sites will be known only to the antiquary and the historian.

CHAPTER IX.

HE BEGINS LIFE ON HIS OWN ACCOUNT,
AND DON'T LIKE IT.

"When my thoughts go back now, to that slow agony of my youth, I wonder how much of the histories I invented, for such people hangs like a mist of fancy over well-remembered facts!"—*David Copperfield*, Chap. XI.

"He was a handsome boy, at that time only twelve years of age."—*Child's History of England*.

SIMULTANEOUSLY with his father's incarceration Charles Dickens was sent to the Blacking manufactory carried on by the Lamerts (James and George) under the name of "Warren." This was a not very successful attempt to rival the extensive business of Robert Warren, of 30, Strand. It was at first established by a

Mr. Jonathan Warren, a relative of Robert Warren, who claimed to have been the original inventor of the blacking recipe ; and, as far as I can ascertain, the two houses appear to have pushed business on precisely the same lines, and to have used the same illustrations, or some of them, to their numerous advertisements.

From fifty to sixty-five years ago these woodcuts were to be seen in all the provincial newspapers of any standing, and the covers of magazines and periodicals were full of them, the blank walls of London and its suburbs, too, were ablaze with their illustrated posters.

But this was at a time when the Trade Marks Acts were unknown, and apparently these rival firms used each others' pictorial devices with impunity.

I give here (see page 75) three of the best known of these engravings (there are many others), and those of my readers who can go back in their memories to the magazine and newspaper literature of sixty years since, will recognise these fac-simile reproductions as old acquaintances. Mr. Forster says, page 50 of vol. i., "they were all very proud, he told me, of the cat scratching the boot, which was their house's device."

I do not propose to dwell upon this period of the boy's life, or to go into any description of his employ-ment ; that "an innocent romantic boy" like Charles

Dickens should have been so utterly thrown away is sad, indeed, but perhaps enough has been said and written on this subject already.

Of these times *David Copperfield* says (Chap. XI.), speaking of himself in the first person, "a child of excellent abilities, and with strong power of observation, quick, eager, delicate, and soon hurt, bodily or mentally, it seems wonderful to me that nobody should have made any sign in my behalf." That he should have escaped serious mental and bodily deterioration during these months is also wonderful!

Most readers of Mr. Forster's *Life* of his friend will, I think, derive satisfaction from these two points: first, that after all, he took some pride in doing the work he was put to thoroughly well ; and, secondly, that at a time when the family circumstances were at a deplorably low ebb, he, a boy of twelve, could, in however wretched a fashion, maintain himself.

Bit by bit all the furniture had been sold, the boy had become familiar with the nature of "pawnbrokers' duplicates—those turnpike tickets on the road of poverty ;"[1] even his favourite books from Chatham had been disposed of, and he now felt the position he had fallen into very keenly ; but it is something to know that, in these dark times, he never quite lost his youthful flow of spirits. Companions suitable to his age and former position he

[1] *Bleak House*, Chap. XI.

STRAND

had none, but he managed to extract some fun both then and afterwards in his works, from the peculiarities of Thomas, the old soldier; of Harry, the good-natured carman; of Mick Walker, of Bob Fagin, and of Poll Green. Of the latter he says, "I think his little sister did imps in the pantomime."

Mr. Forster tells us, "I perfectly recollect that he used to describe Saturday night as his great treat. It was a grand thing to walk home with six shillings in his pocket, and to look in at the shop windows, and think what it would buy."

Hunt's roasted corn, as "a British and patriotic substitute for coffee," was in vogue just then (1824), and this he occasionally purchased; it was another of the curiosities advertised pretty freely in those days, and had an extensive sale for a time, and then came to an end. He used also to purchase *The Portfolio*, which he had a great fancy for taking home with him. This was a weekly illustrated periodical, which would be a great treat to an imaginative boy. It commenced in the year 1823, and the title-page was in this wise, "The Portfolio of Entertaining and Instructive Varieties in History, Science, Literature, the Fine Arts, etc. Price Twopence." *The Portfolio* bore a strong resemblance to *The Mirror. The Vehicle*, and several other magazines started about the same time; it had an existence of about three years' duration, and then it, too, came to an end.

Some of the pieces in *The Portfolio* were burlesques of well-known plays, and outrageous parodies of poems. There is, I fancy, internal evidence in some of Dickens' very earliest printed works, of his having studied these burlesques and travesties to some purpose. There is still stronger evidence of this study, I am told, in some other early attempts of his that were never printed.

It was probably at the end of the year 1824 that Fanny Dickens received a prize at the Royal Academy of Music, and Charles and some others of the family attended at Tenterden Street, to witness the presentation. I have been unable to fix the date of this presentation, as no record of it exists in the books of the Academy. Mr. Forster mentions this event, and adds that in a fragment of autobiography Dickens has remarked on the presentation, " I could not bear to think of myself— beyond the reach of all such honourable emulation and success. The tears ran down my face. I felt as if my heart were rent. I prayed when I went to bed that night to be lifted out of the humiliation and neglect in which I was. I never had suffered so much before. There was no envy in this." And, adds Mr. Forster, with a generous word for his friend, " there was little need that he should say so."

There is no record of the duration of this period of the boy's life, but the date of his father's petition is

May 4th, 1824, and the first hearing was on Thursday, May 27th, of the same year.

His own account of it is, " I have no idea how long it lasted, whether for a year, or much more, or less." That it terminated soon after his father's release is certain, so that the probability is that little Charles Dickens was employed at the blacking warehouse for less than one year, and that he left it somewhere in the summer of 1824.

It is a curious fact, and one to reflect on, that, knowing as the reading world does from Mr. Forster's book, how strongly and enduringly Dickens was affected by these sad times, we yet find him, in nearly all his books, from the very first to the last, continually recurring to the subject of the blacking business.

This topic seems constantly to have forced itself upon him, and to have had a certain fascination for him, which he could not resist. Taking his works in their order of publication, I find he mentions in his *Sketches by Boz* the shabby genteel man in the Seven Dials, who wrote poems for ".Warren." It is mentioned twice in *Pickwick*, once in *Oliver Twist*, in *Nicholas Nickleby* several times, and notably in Chapter XL.; it occurs in the *Old Curiosity Shop*, where Mr. Slum, the writer of poetical advertisements, is introduced. In *David Copperfield* it is veiled under cover of the Wine Stores. In *Hard Times*, where Josiah Bounderby brags that the only pictures he possessed when a boy were the illustrated labels " of a man shaving himself in a boot on the blacking bottles." In *Little Dorrit*, in *Great Expectations*, in *Our Mutual Friend*, and in *Edwin Drood*, are also to be found brief but unmistakable allusions to this business.

At this time Charles was living in Lant Street, in the Borough, where he continued to lodge till his father's affairs were arranged, and the family, after a brief sojourn in Little College Street, went to reside in Johnson Street, between Seymour Street and Old St. Pancras Church.

CHAPTER X.

SCHOOL AGAIN.

"My school-days! The silent gliding on of my existence —the unseen, unfelt progress of my life—from Childhood up to Youth! Let me think, as I look back upon that flowing water, now a dry channel overgrown with leaves, whether there are any marks along its course, by which I can remember how it ran."

David Copperfield, Chap. XVIII.

IN *David Copperfield* the boy terminates his sordid uncongenial drudgery by running away, and, knowing what we now do of the facts, the direction of his flight (Kent) appears to be quite sufficiently accounted for. But in the case of Charles Dickens himself, he was removed from the Blacking Warehouse by his father, and sent to school again for about two years.

G

From data given in the last chapter, he must have been a little over twelve years of age when he entered the school of Mr. Jones, known as the Wellington House Academy, Granby Street, Mornington Place, Hampstead Road. " It was a school of some celebrity in its neighbourhood, nobody could have said why. The master was supposed among us to know nothing, and one of the ushers was supposed to know everything. We are still inclined to think the first-named supposition perfectly correct."

There is probably, in the description of *Our School*, an intentional mixing up of some of his earlier recollections of the school life at Chatham, with the more recent experiences at Wellington House Academy. At this latter school we are told " the boys trained the mice " (white mice) " better than the master trained the boys." This refers to the very lax discipline which obtained in the school, as may be inferred from the fact that all sorts of small animals were kept as pets in the school desks.

The master, however, appears to have made up for laxity in almost every other direction by soundly thrashing the boys on the merest pretext, and a thick mahogany ruler was as often as not the weapon used. But the day scholars, of which Charles Dickens was one, generally escaped these visitations, from a wholesome fear of the wrath of the parents.

There is, no doubt, a reminiscence of Wellington House Academy, in the Salem House of *David Copperfield*, and Mr. Creakle probably stands for the irate Welshman, Mr. Jones. There would also seem to be some reference to this school in *The Schoolboy's Story*, where "Old Cheeseman" (the name of a veritable schoolfellow at Chatham) is introduced. Old Cheeseman had to remain at school during the holidays. "But he was a favourite in general. Once a subscription was raised for him, and to keep up his spirits he was presented before the holidays with two white mice, a rabbit, a pigeon, and a beautiful puppy. Old Cheeseman cried about it —especially soon afterwards, when they all eat one another."

Something of the feeling described in *Copperfield* must have been experienced by Charles Dickens, when he, fresh from the society of Bob Fagin, Poll Green, and the others, was first sent to Wellington House Academy, and the company of respectable middle-class boys. " I was so conscious of having passed through scenes of which they could have no knowledge, and of having acquired experiences foreign to my age, appearance, and condition as one of them, that I half believed it was an imposture to come there as an ordinary little schoolboy. My mind ran upon what they would think, if they knew of my familiar acquaintance with the King's Bench Prison."[1]

[1] *David Copperfield*, Chap. XVI.

But if this was so at first we have the direct assurance of Mr. Owen P. Thomas, his schoolfellow, that he soon recovered his youthful spirits, and, says Mr. Thomas (Forster, vol. i., page 58), "He usually held his head more erect than lads ordinarily do, and there was a general smartness about him."

WELLINGTON HOUSE ACADEMY, HAMPSTEAD ROAD.

To Mr. Thomas, and the two other gentlemen mentioned below (all of whom are still resident in London), I am indebted for the following original information as to these school-days at Wellington House Academy. A view of the school-house, as it still stands, is given here from a sketch by Mr. Edward Hull, and it is noteworthy that George Cruikshank, the eminent artist, lived for many years, and died in one of the houses in the row to the right of the engraving.

Dr. Henry Danson thinks that Dickens " was there two years, viz., during 1824 and 1825, and that he left the school at Christmas of the last-named year. He was my schoolfellow during the whole of that period." Dr. Danson also tells us in Forster, vol. i., page 62, that " he was a handsome, curly-headed lad, full of animation and animal spirits, and probably was connected with every mischievous prank in the school."

Mr. Thomas writes as to the date of Dickens leaving this school : " I have referred to a memorandum-book, now literally in its ' sere and yellow leaf,' belonging to my grandfather, Owen Peregrine, by whom I was brought up, wherein is entered that I ' went to Mr. Jones's school, February 22nd, 1824.' C. Dickens (as he has since told me) was not there then, but came very soon after. So that you may take it as certain that C. D. became a scholar there during that spring.

" I am sorry I cannot fix upon the exact month, but it would not be *later* than June of that year (1824). I was C. Dickens' senior in age by a few months."

I am also indebted to Mr. Thomas for the following diagrams of the school itself.

REFERENCE TO DIAGRAM.

No. 1—Mr. Jones's desk, " the chief."

  " 2—Mr. Manville's do., Latin, etc., Master.

  " 3—Mr. Taylor's   do., English, etc.

  " 4—Mr. Shier's   do., Junior.

           and near him the French Master's chair.

  " 5—Charles Dickens sat about here.*

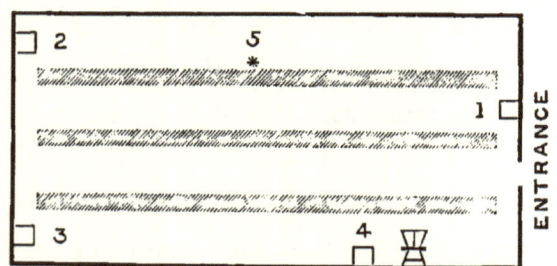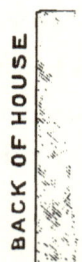

PLAN OF SCHOOLROOM.

No. 1 is described in *Our School* as "the chief."

  " 2 the "Latin master" with "ends of flannel, etc.,"
rather coloured, as C. D. himself remarked
to me, Mr. Manville was then but a middle-
aged man at most.

  " 3 described as the "Clerical looking young man," he
appears also in *David Copperfield.* I think
Mr. Jones was the "Creakle," and other
severe schoolmasters in C. D.'s books. The
boys sat on *each* side of the desks, which were
continuous, but most of them had locked up
portions to themselves."

Mr. Thomas further says the "sketches give an accurate idea of our departed schoolroom, which, I think, was a timber structure, standing in a rather large playground, and parallel with Granby Street, and a little space behind Mr. Jones's house, which latter remains in its original state. I am glad you secured a view of the house. I suggested this to Mr. Forster, but when, I believe, it was too late.

"C. Dickens, the Dansons, Tobin, Bray, and myself were all day-scholars; Bowden was a boarder. Amongst

ELEVATION OF SCHOOLROOM FRONTING GRANBY STREET.

the boarders were the three Keys, and their sisters, mulattos, the latter, of course, under Mrs. Jones's care. They were the children, it was understood, of parents who resided in the East Indies.[1] One of the boys, Frederick, had repeated experiences of the severe scourgings Mr. Jones was so prone to administer."

"It was only on my accidentally finding his juvenile note (printed by Forster, vol. i., 59), that I was led to think the then renowned author was the same I had formerly known so well, and this, strangely enough,

[1] The brother and sister Landless, introduced in *Edwin Drood*, are very probably a recollection of the Keys.

happened to Dr. Danson as well. When I at length met him again, I found him as agreeable and friendly as he had been so many years before as a boy. Mr. Dickens intimated to me, when speaking of our old school, that it had been in his power to render service to Mr. Jones, as well as to Mr. Manville.

" Mr. D. *never* omitted anything it was in his power to do for old friends, ' he was a man, take him for all in all ' that we shall (hardly) ' look upon his like again.'

" I do not remember the exact house in Johnson Street (where C. D. lived at this time), but Dr. Danson believes that it is only a few doors from Seymour Street; he remembers, with C. D., searching a cupboard in the front parlour for a book, probably the pamphlet I had lent him, and which, in the note to me, he says he will send by Harry (Dr. Danson) to-morrow.' The ' Leg ' mentioned is the legend of something just referred to, but we have never been able to understand the exact meaning of ' I have weighed yours every Saturday night.'

" I rather differ from Dr. Danson when he says that C. D. did not, he believes, learn Latin there, because all the senior boys (and C. D. became one) learned the elements of that language, or at least, were supposed to do so, there being an efficient Master always."

Mr. Jno. W. Bowden, another schoolfellow at Wellington House, believes " it was the year 1827, when Dickens left Mr. Jones's Academy. He and I occupied adjoining desks, and I remember we jointly used to issue,—written on scraps of copy-book paper—almost weekly, what we called *Our Newspaper*, lending it to read on payment of marbles, and pieces of slate pencil This paper used to contain sundry bits of boyish fun— the following I recollect—

> '*Lost.* Out of a gentleman's waistcoat pocket, an acre of land ; the finder shall be rewarded on restoring the same.'

> '*Lost.* By a boy with a long red nose, and grey eyes, a very bad temper. Whoever has found the same may keep it, as the owner is better without it.'

" The ' Lingo ' mentioned by Mr. Forster, as being invented by Dickens, was what we call *gibberish*, and was spoken before Dickens came to the school. The view you send (of the school-house) is very correct."

Mr. Bowden says that Mr. Taylor, the English master, " who was a constant flute-player,"[1] left Mr. Jones, and opened a school for himself, known as " the Retreat, South Lambeth," and that Charles Dickens went to this school for some time. He says also that at Wellington House, music was taught in the front room on the ground floor, and here he himself and Charles Dickens received lessons on the violin, which study Dickens could by no means make any progress in, and had to relinquish.

---

[1] The original, probably, of *Mr. Mell* in *David Copperfield*.

Among his schoolfellows at this time was (according to Dr. Danson) a Master Beverley, afterwards the great scene painter, and his early artistic efforts were now utilised to paint scenic effects for the boys' theatres. There cannot be a doubt that, under the joint management of two such boys as Dickens and Beverley these theatrical performances must have been considerably in advance of the ordinary juvenile theatricals to be then found in schools !

While at Wellington House (where all sorts of mechanical ingenuities were practised by the boys) Charles Dickens is not likely to have learned a great deal, certainly not much of Latin or Greek, or indeed of many other things that in these days of educational pressure are thought to be absolutely indispensable. This has been disparagingly commented on by some, but there are those who think that, on the whole, it is better for the world at large that things were as they were.

Charles Dickens was learning all the time, and few indeed have put their knowledge of human nature (forced on them by " harsh evidence " in their youth) to a better purpose ! The works of Dickens have done more to perpetuate kindly feelings between rich and poor " than half the homilies that have ever been written by half the Divines that have ever lived." [1]

At this school, we are told, Tales and Plays were

[1] *Sketches by Boz.* A Christmas Dinner.

written, recited, and performed, and the current works of fiction eagerly sought after and studied by "a sort of club" consisting of some of the older boys.

In *Our School*, which is supposed to represent generally the school of Mr. Jones in the Hampstead Road, mention is made of "a serving man, whose name was Phil." This oddity was really in existence at Chatham in the Ordnance Terrace days, where he was well known. He afterwards appears as Phil Squod in *Bleak House !* In *Our School* it is said of him "when we had the scarlet fever in the school, Phil nursed all the sick boys of his own accord, and was like a mother to them." The reader will remember, too, how in *Bleak House*, Chap. XLVII., Phil Squod nursed the poor crossing-sweeper, " Jo," in his last illness.

One of the ushers from Mr. Wm. Jones' Academy afterwards became tutor to Mr. Macready's son, and to this fact, says Mr. Forster, " Dickens used to point for one of the illustrations of his favourite theory as to the smallness of the world, and how things and persons apparently the most unlikely to meet were continually knocking up against each other." Or, as Dickens himself says in *Bleak House*, Chap. XVI., " What connection can there have been between many people in the innumerable histories of this world, who, from opposite sides of great gulfs, have, nevertheless, been very curiously brought together ? "

Charles Dickens appears, then, to have left Wellington House Academy in 1826, and though in the first edition of this work (following Mr. Forster's *Life of Charles Dickens*, vol. i.) it was stated that he afterwards, "probably for a few months only," went to another school in Brunswick Square, it has since been conclusively shown that Wellington House Academy was Dickens' last school.

His younger brothers however, were at Mr. Danson's, the Brunswick Square School, with Thomas Mitton, who thus became acquainted with Charles Dickens.

Mr. Owen P. Thomas writes me under date May 6th, 1885, and speaking of one of his interviews with his illustrious schoolfellow in after life, he says, " I put the question to him whether he went to any other school after leaving Mr. Jones', and he said ' No.' "

CHAPTER XI.

IN THE LAW.

"I am not in a condition to report further of him than that he had the sprightly bearing of a lawyer's clerk."

Uncommercial Traveller. TITBULL'S.

"Though necessity has no law, she has her lawyers."

Old Curiosity Shop, Chap. LXVI.

SOON after leaving school Charles was for a short time employed as clerk to a Mr. Molloy, a solicitor in New Square, Lincoln's Inn Fields, and young Mitton, "Dear Tom," as he was afterwards addressed in many admirable letters, was with him at this time. It cannot but be interesting to know that little more than ten years after his being a fellow-clerk with Thomas

Mitton, he instructed his old friend to make his will for him, on his undertaking a journey into the North of England by coach. The date of the letter is simply 1838, without month or day of month, and he concludes thus, "and so pray God that you may be gray, and Forster bald, long before you are called upon to act as my executors."

At a later date (1844) some of his most brilliant letters from Italy were addressed to Mr. Mitton.

I cannot fix any precise date for his leaving school, nor for the time of his entering or quitting Mr. Molloy's employ, but his next appointment to a clerkship in a lawyer's office can fortunately be fixed with accuracy. He was fifteen years and three months old when he entered the office of Mr. Edward Blackmore, attorney, of Gray's Inn, in May 1827, and nearly seventeen years of age when he left in November 1828.

During these eighteen months Charles Dickens must have seen a great deal of the ordinary routine of a lawyer's office, and accordingly we have throughout his works lawyers of almost every possible shade and variety, from Mr. Sampson Brass to Mr. Tulkinghorn, and from Solomon Pell to Mr. Grewgious.

Of firms of solicitors besides those introduced into the tales, such as Snitchey and Craggs, Dodson and Fogg, Kenge and Carboys, and others, are some highly characteristic names of firms incidentally mentioned in

Pickwick, where at Serjeants' Inn they were called out as it were antiphonally, in tenor and bass voices, "Sniggle and Blink, Porkin and Snob, Stumpy and Deacon!"

Of lawyers' clerks there are "the managing clerk, common-law clerk, conveyancing clerk, chancery clerk, every refinement and department of clerk,"[1] from Mr. Lowten to Dick Swiveller, and from John Wemmick to young Blight. Of the numerous *Dickens books* to be written hereafter, it requires no spirit of prophecy to perceive that this attractive subject, *The Lawyers of Dickens and their Clerks*, will most certainly be undertaken by some one.

From first entering a solicitor's office the prospects of Charles Dickens were improving; he was now entering upon life in earnest, and it may be said of him from this time that "his life lay fair before him."[2] For the study of the peculiar phases of English manners which he has everywhere in his books so happily pourtrayed, he could not well have been more advantageously placed. It was in Mr. Edward Blackmore's offices, we are expressly told by that gentleman in Forster (vol. i., page 67), that some of the incidents took place which are mentioned in *Pickwick* and *Nickleby*, and, says Mr. Blackmore, "I am much mistaken if

[1] *Our Mutual Friend*, vol. i., p. 65. See also *Pickwick Papers*, Chap. XXXI.

[2] *Child's History of England*, Chap. XII.

some of his characters had not their originals in persons I well remember."

There can be no doubt of this, but who the persons were that Mr. Blackmore alludes to, and what were the incidents mentioned as having transpired in his office, we shall probably never know.

It must have been chiefly during these months at the office in Gray's Inn, that Charles Dickens made his early acquaintance with the ins and outs of London life, and that he acquired that wonderfully accurate knowledge of London itself, which, when published as *Sketches by Boz*, suddenly astonished the reading world of 1834-5-6.

But whether in the lawyer's office, the minor theatres (where he is said occasionally to have taken parts), or in the streets of London, his keen faculty of observation was now in the fullest activity, " I looked at nothing that I know of, but I saw everything," says David Copperfield for Charles Dickens, Chap. XXVII.

Charles had probably been but a short time in the attorney's office, when he began to seek other more congenial and remunerative employment. He was quick to see that his prospects of gaining honourable distinction in life did not lie in the way of the mere drudgery of a clerk of whatever grade, and he sought to add to his income by qualifying himself as a short-hand writer to report law cases in the courts.

This at first was what he had in his mind, and so we see that his *double* Copperfield speaks for him thus in Chap. XXXVI. : " I'll buy a book," said I, " with a good scheme of this art in it ; I'll work at it at the Commons, where I haven't half enough to do ; I'll take down the speeches in our court for practice."

So " I bought an approved scheme of the noble art and mystery of stenography (which cost me ten-and-six-pence), and plunged into a sea of perplexity that brought me in a few weeks to the confines of distraction." This book was *Gurney's Brachygraphy ; or, an Easy and Compendious System of Shorthand,* 15th edition, 1824.

The difficulties of thoroughly mastering this system as Dickens mastered it, are scarcely exaggerated in the tale, and were far greater than in the more modern system of phonography now very generally used by the most expert parliamentary reporters.

As these studies were going on during the greater part of the time he was a clerk or office boy, he could not obviously have given much of his spare time to theatri-cals, private or otherwise, nor to any of those cheap enjoyments which were and are so much sought after by very many youths in his position.

During the latter year of his time with Mr. Blackmore, that is in the year 1828, Charles had a brief holiday, and visited some old friends of his family residing at Luton, near Chatham, and there is a sort of traditional

II

recollection of this visit still remaining in the neigh-bourhood.

The *New York Tribune* is responsible for the following anecdote, which is probably strictly true, the more so as it confirms the story of Charles Dickens revisiting the scenes of his childhood in this year, and as it is itself confirmed by a short article in *Good Words* for July 1882. The anecdote from the *New York Tribune* is this :—

"The late Dr. John Brown, when a young man, spent a year as an assistant-surgeon at Chatham, with which place Charles Dickens had so many associations.

"Many years after the Doctor met the novelist for the first and only time, and, the conversation turning on nationalities, Dickens said that he had been cured of any cockney prejudice against Scotchmen which he might have had by the heroic conduct of a young Scotch surgeon which he had witnessed at Chatham during the time of cholera.

"Strange, to say, this young surgeon was none other than the friend to whom he was telling the story."

The article in *Good Words*, from which the following is extracted, was written by Walter C. Smith, D.D., and is a sketch of the life of Dr. Brown :—

"When he was some eighteen years old (1828), for in those days university education began with boys of twelve or thirteen, he went up to Chatham as assistant to a surgeon or physician there, and remained a year, brightening, I daresay, many a sick bed by his sweet boyish face, and his gaiety and sympathy."

This Dr. Brown was the well known charming writer, the author of *Rab and his Friends*, etc.

Although he was now, as Mr. Forster says, merely "one of the office lads," Charles Dickens was no doubt employed for part, at least, of his time, in copying documents, and most likely sometimes in serving process.

His knowledge of law terms and expressions is everywhere seen in his books, and if we knew nothing of his early history it would surely strike even careless readers of Dickens that he must at some time have been in a lawyer's office himself.

But he was now about to try a complete change of employment, and in the next chapter it will be seen that he had during these later months been steadily acquiring the means of bettering his position in the world,—had, in fact, been bettering his position all the time.

[1] See also another account of this incident in *The Century* illustrated monthly magazine for December 1882.

CHAPTER XII.

REPORTING AND WRITING FOR MAGAZINES.

"I have tamed that savage stenographic mystery."
David Copperfield, Chap. XLIII.

"Night after night I record predictions that never come to pass, professions that are never fulfilled, explanations that are only meant to mystify."—*Ibid*.

CLEAR of the valley of the shadow of the Law, Charles Dickens applied himself with his customary energy and intensity of will, to the practice of shorthand writing and reporting as a means of livelihood. He was now seventeen, and his first employment as a reporter was in the Lord Chancellor's

Court taking notes of the cases, and here Mr. Blackmore, the solicitor, says he occasionally saw him after he left his service.

Of the Law itself, apart from the administration of it, he seems to have held at no period of his life any very high opinion, and his experience of the utterances it was his duty to record in the various courts (the Admiralty, the Arches, and the Prerogative Courts amongst the number) did not, as may be readily inferred from a study of his works, impress him very favourably with the majesty of the Law. A passage from a letter to Mrs. Frederick Pollock, written late in life,[1] seems to uphold this view : " I have that high opinion of the law of England generally, which one is likely to derive from the impression that it puts all the honest men under the diabolical hoofs of all the scoundrels."

At Doctors' Commons he is said to have practised stenography for nearly two years, but there is no doubt that, during this period, he also reported police cases in the various Metropolitan Police Courts.

In the first volume of the *Life of Charles Dickens*, Mr. Forster gives a detailed account of the difficulties that had to be overcome, and the time that had to be spent, before his friend could sufficiently master the mysteries of his new calling, to ensure him employment as an efficient verbatim reporter. He closes a rather

[1] Monday, May 2nd, 1870. (*Vide Letters of Charles Dickens*, vol. ii.)

long sentence on page 69 thus, " his father already having taken to it (reporting) in these latter years, in aid of the family resources."

It is true Mr. Forster was not writing the life of John Dickens, but one naturally wonders (if it was so difficult a task for a young man) how the father, now arrived at middle age, could so readily have acquired the art of reporting ! !

The fact that Mr. John Dickens could and did, at the age of forty-five, take up with a new and difficult study, and attain a place in the Reporters' Gallery of the House of Commons, as one of the staff of a daily paper, is, to say the least, a convincing proof of his energy and application, and is, I think, deserving of being recorded with some emphasis in any worthy biography of his talented son !

During these earlier reporting days the name of Charles Dickens is first found in the books of The British Museum. He read there for the first time on the 8th February, 1830, aged eighteen, and is described as then living at No. 10, Norfolk Street, Fitzroy Square. In the reading-room books he is further described, on the 2nd February, 1833, as of 18, Bentinck Street, Cavendish Square.

It cannot fail to interest the reader to know that he attended the British Museum as a reader the day after he had attained the then prescribed age—viz., eighteen.

Young Dickens was from this time a frequent and most eager student at the reading room, and it is certain that he not only greatly benefited by his reading there, but that, to have the resources of a noble library, " rich with the stores of time " at his command, was to him a constant and increasing source of delight.[1]

The first parliamentary reporting of Charles Dickens was on his being appointed to a seat in the gallery, as one of the staff of the *True Sun*, a paper with which Mr. Forster was intimately connected, and to which he contributed articles ; and it was at the office of this paper that a friendship commenced which, stretching over a third of a century, terminated only with the life of Dickens. Mr. Forster says that there was at this time a strike of the reporters of their paper, and that Dickens, a youth of nineteen, was chosen by the reporters as their spokesman, " and conducted their case triumphantly !"

It may be noted here that, speaking of his early reporting days at the Newspaper-press Fund dinner, May 20th, 1865, he says, " I went into the gallery of the House of Commons as a parliamentary reporter when I was a boy not eighteen, and I left it—I can hardly believe the inexorable truth—nigh thirty years ago."

---

[1] Mr. W. B. Rye says in answer to a question as to what books Dickens read at this time : " There is now no possibility of ascertaining at the British Museum what books C. D. used when a reader ; no record was kept of these until many years afterwards. In all probability they were books on *Shorthand*, which C. D. then assiduously set to work to acquire."

I am not able to fix any date for his ceasing to report for the *True Sun,* nor for his commencing an engagement on the staff of his maternal uncle's paper, *The Mirror of Parliament,* but it was probably in the year 1832.

The Mirror of Parliament has been described by several writers as " short lived " and " ephemeral," but a paper that lasts through ten sessions of Parliament, and a corresponding number of years, can scarcely be correctly said to have had a " brief life ! ! "

The Mirror of Parliament commenced on the 29th January, 1828, and was originated and edited by John Henry Barrow, Esq.,[1] of the Honourable Society of Gray's Inn, barrister-at-law, and was first published by Messrs. Winchester and Varnham, of 61, Strand. It went steadily on till the end of the session of 1837, when it collapsed, the publishing office at the close of its career being at 3, Abingdon Street, Westminster. From an examination of all the volumes, the reports of the speeches seem to have been unusually full for the date at which they were printed, and to have been faithfully and carefully done.

In his monograph of Charles Dickens (1870) Mr. G. A. Sala says : " In his time Charles Dickens must have

---

[1] John Henry Barrow was one of the witnesses to the marriage of his sister Mary, at Chatham, in 1821. (See *ante,* Chap. VI.) His *Mirror of Parliament* was originally published by subscription.

listened to and taken down the words of the speeches of nearly every public man of the last generation. He reported Brougham's great speech at Edinburgh, after his resignation of the Chancellorship. He may have reported Lord Stanley's famous oration on the Irish Church. He must have reported habitually the speeches of Peel and Grey, of Denman, of Lyndhurst, of Ellenborough, of Hume, and Melbourne, and Grote."

"Twenty years after he left the gallery he retained enough of his ancient craft to teach the art of shorthand very thoroughly and completely to a young brother-in-law, who was entering on the career of journalism."

While still busy reporting for his uncle's *Mirror of Parliament*, and when just turned twenty-one years of age, he wrote for performance among the members of his own family a sort of travesty of *Othello*. For the following literary curiosity I am indebted to Mr. W. B. Rye, and to Mr. S. Dyer Knott, of Alphington, near Exeter, who kindly allowed Mr. Rye to transcribe and in part trace the fragment now printed for the first time.

Mr. Knott was a neighbour of Mr. John Dickens when the latter lived at Mile-end Cottage,[1] Alphington, in 1842, and had many a friendly chat with him. This

---

[1] It is a curious coincidence that, when Charles was born, his father was living at *Mile-end* Terrace, Portsea (see *ante*).

was just after the publication of *Nicholas Nickleby*. He remembers also his son Augustus, and more than once saw the great humourist at Alphington, when on a visit to his father.

Mr. Knott describes Mr. John Dickens " as a chatty, pleasant companion, possessing a varied fund of anecdote, and a genuine vein of humour. He was a well-built man, rather stout, of very active habits, a little pompous, and very proud (as well he might be) of his talented son. He dressed well, and wore a goodly bunch of seals suspended across his waistcoat from his watch-chain." [1]

Of the travesty two pages numbered 1 and 2, at the bottom of the MS., were given to Mr. Knott by Mr. John Dickens, who has placed his name and the date in the corner. How many folios of this production were given to other friends it would be hard to tell, but I have direct evidence that other portions of it are in existence at the present time !

The extract given here will serve to show the hand-writing of Dickens at this early age ; it very closely resembles the manuscript of *Oliver Twist*, and contrasts strangely with the portion of *Edwin Drood*, given in *fac-simile*, in the third volume of Mr. Forster's *Life of Charles Dickens*, page 430.

---

[1] Note by Mr. Rye.

Sutherland
Applington / 7 July 1842

Solo — Cantis
Aria — " When in death I shall calm recline."

=

When in death I shall calm recline,
Oh! take me home to my Susan "dear;"
Tell her I've taken a little more wine
Than I could carry, or very well bear;

FRAGMENT OF MS. TO SHOW HANDWRITING AT THE AGE OF 21.

SOLO—CASSIO.

———

Air—" When in death I shall calm recline."[1]

When in sleep I shall calm recline,
 Oh ! take me home to my " missus " dear ;
Tell her I've taken a little more wine
 Than I could carry, or very well bear ;
Bid her not scold me on the morrow
 For staying out drinking all the night ;
But several bottles of soda borrow,
 To cool my coppers and set me right.

It was not till his twenty-third year that he became a reporter on the staff of the *Morning Chronicle*, and by all obtainable accounts he was then at the very head of his profession ; he is said, indeed, to have been the best reporter of his time.

In *David Copperfield* (Chap. XLIII.) he says : " I have come out in another way. I have taken with fear and trembling to authorship. I wrote a little something, in secret, and sent it to a magazine, and it was published in the magazine."

It was while still acting as a reporter on the *Morning Chronicle* that the first of his *Sketches* was published in the December number of the *Monthly Magazine* for 1833. It was entitled " A Dinner at Poplar Walk ;"[2]

[1] Moore's *Melodies*.
[2] Afterwards (in the collected *Sketches*) entitled " Mr. Minns and his Cousin."

and we read in Mr. Forster's book, vol. i., page 76, how the young author purchased a copy of this number at a shop in the Strand, and " walked down to Westminster Hall, and turned into it for half an hour, because his eyes were so dimmed with joy and pride, that they could not bear the street, and were not fit to be seen there."

On referring to these old volumes of the *Monthly Magazine*, I find the first *Sketch*, " A Dinner at Poplar Walk," commences on page 617, and the cousin's name is there given as Bagshaw ; this became Budden in the collected volume of *Sketches*. There are in it also some other minor alterations. The second *Sketch* appeared in the January number for 1834, and is called " Mrs. Joseph Porter over the Way." This was followed by " Horatio Sparkins " in February, " The Bloomsbury Christening " in April, the first part of " The Boarding House " in May, and the second part, signed " Boz," in August, followed by " The Steam Excursion " in October.

Charles Dickens, after some eight or ten of these had appeared, continued the series in the *Evening Chronicle*.

It was in this evening paper, and under the name of " Boz," that he scored his first great success ; and from these early days, even while still engaged as a reporter in the gallery of the House of Commons, there was for the young author really no looking back !

Dr. Johnson tells us, solemnly enough,

" Slow rises worth by poverty depress'd,"

but his "mournful truth" was altogether without force in the case of Charles Dickens; for even in these pre-Pickwick times the *Sketches* had achieved a wide popularity, a popularity the more remarkable, for the reason that the subjects written about, and still more, the manner of treating them, had attracted *all classes* of the reading public, while as yet no one knew who the brilliant writer was.

> Who the dickens " Boz " could be
> Puzzled many a curious elf,
> Till time unveiled the mystery,
> And " Boz " appeared as Dickens' self.
> *Bentley's Miscellany*, No. 2, March 1837.

The account in Mr. Forster's *Life of Charles Dickens* of the origin of the word " Boz " is no doubt correct, and the fact of Dickens having adopted as his own the pet name of a younger brother, is an additional and interesting proof of his love for all recollections of his early years, and for the associations of home.

It cannot now be necessary to point out the vast renown that immediately fell to the lot of the young writer, for it has been thoroughly well done over and over again.

" Here was a young man," says Mr. G. A. Sala, "as destitute of a patron as he was of a degree, who suddenly uprose and took the literary world by storm."

The brilliant circle that now opened to Dickens might

very excusably have turned an older head, but, in his case, it is on record that through the whole of his literary career, extending over a period of more than thirty-six years, he was unspoiled to a wonderful degree, and remained so to the last.

This concludes my brief sketch of the early life of Charles Dickens ; it will be seen that, in this history, I have taken very little on trust, but have, so far as practicable, gone to head-quarters for every scrap of information that would be likely to interest the reader.

After giving in the next chapter some account of Gad's Hill, past and present, I shall endeavour to point out, in a series of notes, some of the more obvious passages in the writings of Charles Dickens, which may be considered to have autobiographical features, and which are undoubtedly reminiscences of his own early recollections and tender youthful experiences.

CHAPTER XIII.

GAD'S HILL.

" This is Falstaff's own Gad's Hill, and I live on the top of it. My eldest daughter keeps my house, and it is one I was extraordinarily fond of when a child."

Letter to the Earl of Carlisle, August 8th, 1860.

" It's a place you may well be fond of, and attached to, for it's the prettiest spot in all the country round."

Village Coquettes, Act III., Scene 1.

 GREAT deal of ingenuity has been wasted by writers on this locality in an endeavour to account for the name GAD'S HILL.[1] There can be and is, however, no doubt that the true derivation is GOD'S HILL. There is, it may be remembered, a parish of this name (God's Hill)

[1] There is another Gad's Hill at Gillingham, near Chatham.

in the Isle of Wight, spelt *Gaddishill*, when referred to in *The Paston Letters*, August 20th, 1499, also a tithing, so called, in the parish of Fordingbridge, co. Southampton.

A passage in the Prayer-Book version of the Psalms will occur to many in this connection, " Why hop ye so, ye high hills ? This is God's Hill, in the which it pleaseth Him to dwell. Yea, the Lord will abide in it for ever."—*Psalm* lxviii. 16.

Gad's Hill is situate on the High Dover Road, and is four and a half miles from Gravesend, and two and a half from Rochester. Here is a pleasant description of its geographical bearings from the *Ingoldsby Penance*, by the Rev. R. H. Barham :—

> " Cobham woods to the right—on the opposite shore
> Laindon Hills in the distance, ten miles off or more ;
> Then you've Milton and Gravesend behind—and before
> You can see almost all the way down to the Nore ;
> ——————So charming a spot it's rarely one's lot
> To see, and when seen it's as rarely forgot."

As a " High old Robbing Hill " (as an early writer describes it), it has long enjoyed a bad eminence, and many notorious robbbers are known to have frequented this spot long before Shakespeare immortalised it in his play of *Henry the Fourth*.

Gad's Hill is also mentioned as a " high place " for robbers in Ben Jonson's *Every Man out of his Humour*, Act IV. Scene 5.

I

A " story is extant," and if not "writ in choice Italian " yet in very quaint English, that, in 1676, at Gad's Hill, one " Swift Nicks," or Nevisham, robbed a gentleman at " four of the clock in the morning," and, passing the Thames by ferry, rode through the day till he came to York in the evening, and presenting himself on a bowling green there, as a place of public resort where his presence would be observed, asked the time of day of the Lord Mayor of the city.[1]

The fact of his being seen at York, at the time named, having been proved on his trial for the robbery, he was acquitted on the ground of its being impossible for a man to ride from Gad's Hill to York in the space of one day. The jury were no doubt right, and the story (like many others of the sort) is probably a mere invention.

But long since Charles the Second's time, and within the last eighty years, Gad's Hill has been a favourite haunt of footpads, their victims being often enough sailors (whether " Mercantile Jack " or man-of-war's man) who having just been paid off at Chatham, were on their way to London, stopped and robbed here.

The natural beauties, commanding position, and romantic history of Gad's Hill would be certain to make

---

[1] For a full account of this robbery see *Records of York Castle*, page 247, also *Pocock's History of Gravesend*, page 245. Nevisham was hanged at York in 1681.

a lasting impression on the mind of any sensitive boy, and that Charles Dickens was from a very tender age so impressed, and that even then he was much attached to the place, we have on record in his own words over and over again.

In his *Life*, and also in his *Letters*, we are told of his occasional visits to this spot, when out for a ramble with his father. That he should have come to be the owner of Gad's Hill Place, and to reside here is, besides

"THERE'S MILESTONES ON THE DOVER ROAD"

being a remarkable coincidence, another instance of the truth of a favourite saying of his as to " the smallness of the world."

In the *Uncommercial Traveller*, chapter on " Tramps," is a wonderfully truthful picture of this spot :—

"I have my eye on a piece of Kentish road, bordered on either side by a wood, and having on one hand, between the road-dust and the trees, a skirting patch of grass. Wild flowers grow in abundance on this spot, and it lies high and airy, with a distant river stealing away to the ocean, like a man's life. To gain the milestone here, which the moss, primroses, violets, blue-bells, and wild-roses would soon render illegible but for peering travellers pushing them aside with their sticks, you must come up a steep hill, come which way you may. So all the tramps with carts or caravans—the gipsy tramp, the show tramp, the Cheap Jack—find it impossible to resist the temptations of the place, and all turn the horse loose when they come to it, and boil the pot. Bless the place, I love the ashes of the vagabond fires that have scorched its grass!

THE FALSTAFF INN, GAD'S HILL.

"Within appropriate distance of this magic ground, though not so near it as that the song trolled from tap or bench at door can invade its woodland silence, is a little hostelry which no man possessed of a penny was ever known to pass in warm weather. Before its entrance are certain pleasant trimmed limes; likewise a cool well, with so musical a bucket-handle that its fall upon the bucket rim will make a horse prick up his ears and neigh, upon the droughty road half a mile off."

This is the Falstaff, a delightfully old-fashioned road-side inn of the coaching days. Although the well and bucket are still there, the limes, with one solitary exception, have disappeared, as has also the quaint swinging sign, representing in impossible colours scenes from *The Merry Wives of Windsor* and *Henry the Fourth*.

In other respects, however, the whole neighbourhood of Gad's Hill is very little changed in forty years, and wayfarers are apparently still unable to pass the old inn without giving a call.

A short distance from this historical tavern, on the north side of the road, on an eminence, stands an obelisk erected some fifty years since to the memory of Charles Larkin, of Rochester. It is of brick, covered with cement, and is a prominent object in the landscape, especially from the lower reaches of the Thames. This monument is incidentally mentioned in a letter to Mr. Wilkie Collins, dated  October 26th, 1860, which see for an amusing account of the laying of a ghost! (*Letters of Charles Dickens*, vol. ii., page 131.)

The neighbourhood of Gad's Hill is, among other pleasant memories, noted for the number and variety of its singing birds, and the glorious voice of the nightingale is heard here in the spring in full perfection.

The house, Gad's Hill Place, now the property of the Hon. Francis Law Latham, is, notwithstanding the large sums of money laid out on it by the late Charles Dickens, much the same in appearance (so far as the front is concerned) as it was forty or fifty years ago. Indeed, but for the rapid growth of his lime trees skirting the road, the place is, as seen by a passing traveller, quite unaltered. Major Budden writes me, and I am sorry to record it, that Dickens' favourite May trees, planted by him in the middle of the meadow at the back of the house, were destroyed by the great gale of wind on the 14th October, 1881.

In the shrubbery, on the opposite side of the road, are the two fine cedars (*Cedrus Libani*), for which the neighbourhood is celebrated. In my recollection these cedars were certainly not half the size they have now attained.

Each tree covers a circular area of about eighty feet diameter.

They are still growing rapidly, and though so very large and fine, were planted when the house was built, by the father of a man still living. Mr. John Brooker, of Higham (in whom one recognises some of the better qualities and peculiarities of Durdles in *Edwin Drood*), told me that his father planted these trees well nigh a hundred years ago, and that they were originally placed there in boxes. Mr. Brooker is halfway between eighty

THE CEDARS, GAD'S HILL.

and ninety years of age, and bears his years wonderfully
well. There can, I think, be no reasonable doubt of the
perfect accuracy of his statement, but nine persons out
of ten would take Brooker to be much younger than he
is, and the trees to be much older than we know they
are !

The engraving gives a good idea of their present
aspect,[1] and the steps leading to the shrubbery can be
seen in the sketch. They are approached by a tunnel
passing under the high road, direct from the lawn in
front of the house.

Behind the shrubs in the north-west corner of these
grounds formerly stood the Swiss châlet (now at Cobham
Hall) presented to Charles Dickens by Mr. Fechter. In
the upper story of this pretty building the last pages of
Edwin Drood were written, and here the great writer's
last quiet hours of consciousness were passed. The
châlet was, as it were, surrounded with and nearly con-
cealed by lofty trees, with an opening only to the
north, and from that side there was one of the finest
views to be found in the county of Kent.

Major Budden, the former owner of Gad's Hill Place,
wrote me that, among the numerous visitors to Gad's
Hill Place, are many Americans, who would consider
their journey to England incomplete without seeing the

[1] Under the spreading boughs of one of the cedars lies "Linda," a
favourite dog.

last residence of their favourite author, Charles Dickens. He adds, "Many people suppose the house is closed to visitors, but it is not really so, and any respectable person wishing to see it will have no difficulty."

In the case of American friends, they will always experience courteous attention and recognition on presenting the card of the American Consul.

In the Library may still be seen the counterfeit book-backs, arranged on shelves to fit the door of the room. An engraving is given here of the general appearance of this door, and a complete list of the titles of the volumes follows. Those distinguished by an asterisk were also used for a similar purpose at Tavistock House, London, and are printed in the *Letters of Charles Dickens*, vol. i., page 266.

*Commonplace Book of the Oldest Inhabitant.   2 vols.
*Growler's Gruffiology, with Appendix.   4 vols.
*The Books of Moses and Sons.   2 vols.
*Burke (of Edinburgh) on the Sublime and Beautiful.   2 vols.
*King Henry the Eighth's Evidences of Christianity.   5 vols.
  Haydn's Commentaries.
*Miss Biffin on Deportment.
*Morrison's Pills Progress.   2 vols.
*Lady Godiva on the Horse.
*Munchausen's Modern Miracles.   4 vols.
*Richardson's Show of Dramatic Literature.   12 vols.

THE DOOR OF LIBRARY, GAD'S HILL PLACE.

*Hansard's Guide to Refreshing Sleep. (Many vols.)

Strutt's Walk.

Socrates on Wedlock.

Optics. (Hooks and Eyes.)

Acoustics. (Cod's Sounds.)

The Locomotive Engine explained by Colonel Sibthorpe.

Catalogue of Statues to the Duke of Wellington. 10 vols

Noah's Arkitecture. 2 vols.

Butcher's Suetonius.

Hoyle on the Turnip.

Critts' Edition of Meller. 2 vols.

The Delphin Oracle.

The Cook's Oracle.

Mag's Diversions. 4 vols.

Drouett's Farming. 5 vols.

Chickweed.

Groundsel. (By the author of Chickweed.)

Cats' Lives. 9 vols.

The Scotch Fiddle. (Burns.)

Shelley's Oysters.

Waterworks. (By Father Matthew.)

Swallows on Emigration. 2 vols.

Cockatoo on Perch.

*Five Minutes in China. 3 vols.

*Abernethy on the Constitution. 2 vols.

*Green's Overland Mail.

*Orson's Art of Etiquette.

Adam's Precedents.

Hudson's Complete Failure.

*Downeaster's Complete Calculator.

*History of the Middling Ages. 6 vols.

*Jonah's Account of the Whale.

*Kant's Eminent Humbugs.   10 vols.

*Bowwowdom.

*The Quarrelly Review.   4 vols.

*The Gunpowder Magazine.   4 vols.

*Steele, by the Author of " Ion."

*The Art of Cutting Teeth.

*Malthus's Nursery Songs.   2 vols.

*Paxton's Bloomers.   5 vols.

*On the Use of Mercury by the Ancient Poets.

*Drowsy's Recollections of Nothing.

   Treatise on the Tapeworm by Tim Bobbin.

*Heavysides Conversations with Nobody.   3 vols.

   Phrenology (Italian Organ).

*Teazer's Commentaries.

   Woods and Forests.   By Peter the Wild Boy.

   The Wisdom of our Ancestors.   I.—Ignorance.   II.—
      Superstition.   III.—The Block.   IV.—The Stake.   V.
      —The Rack.   VI.—Dirt.   VII.—Disease.

   General Tom Thumb's Modern Warfare.   2 vols.

   Was Shakespeare's Mother Fair ?   4 vols.

   Had Shakespeare's Uncle a singing Face ?   5 vols.

   Was Shakespeare's Father Merry?   6 vols.

   The Pleasures of Boredom.   (A Poem.)

   History of a Short Chancery Suit.   21 vols.

*Forty Winks at the Pyramids.   2 vols.

*Captain Cook's Life of Savage.   2 vols.

*A Carpenter's Bench of Bishops.   2 vols.

*Toot's Universal Letter-Writer.   2 vols.

   Life and Letters of the Learned Pig.

*Captain Parry's Virtues of Cold Tar.

On Monday, September 3rd, 1860, Charles Dickens

made a remarkable bonfire at Gad's Hill, a bare recital of which will be read with regret by those who can recall the many illustrious correspondents whose letters must then have fed the flames. A mere list of their names would, if closely printed, fill several of these pages.

In a letter to Mr. W. H. Wills, from *All the Year Round* Office, dated Tuesday, September 4th, 1860, he thus describes the immolation :—

"Yesterday I burnt in the field, at Gad's Hill, the accumulated letters and papers of twenty years. They sent up a smoke like the Genie when he got out of the casket on the sea-shore, and as it was an exquisite day when I began, and rained very heavily when I finished, I suspect my correspondence of having overcast the face of the heavens."

Letter to Macready, March 1st, 1865 :—

"My reply to Professor Agassiz is short, but conclusive. Daily seeing improper uses made of confidential letters in addressing them to a public audience that have no business with them, I made, not long ago, a great fire in my field at Gad's Hill, and burnt every letter. I possessed. And now I always destroy every letter I receive not on absolute business, and my mind is so far at ease. Poor dear Felton's letters went up into the air with the rest, or his highly distinguished representative should have had them most willingly."

In Mr. O'Driscoll's *Life of Maclise*, he says, in the

Preface, he received the following letter from Charles Dickens a few days before his lamented death :—

> " GAD'S HILL PLACE, HIGHAM BY ROCHESTER,
> " *Wednesday, May* 18*th,* 1870.

" MY DEAR SIR,—I beg to assure you, in reply to your letter, that I have not one solitary scrap of the late Mr. Maclise's handwriting in my possession. A few years ago I destroyed an immense correspondence, expressly because I considered it had been held with me, and not with the public, and *because I could not answer for its privacy being respected when I should be dead.*"

It is impossible, however, to escape the reflection that, had others made similar bonfires, where would have been the three charming volumes of *The Letters of Charles Dickens ?*

A friend [1] has sent me a printed broadside of some sports held at Gad's Hill Place, December 26th, 1866. It appears to have been a programme of one part only of the day's amusements, and reveals internal evidence of having been the work of some young but ardent amateur printer. The sports were held on this occasion in the field at the back of the house, and Mr. Trood, the then landlord of the Falstaff, had, by permission of the generous owner, a booth erected in the field for the refreshment of the crowds of people who attended the games :—

[1] Mr. Charles Bullard, of Rochester, since dead.

CHRISTMAS SPORTS.

THE ALL COMERS' RACE.

Distance—Once round the field.

First Prize, 10s. ; Second, 5s. ; Third, 2s. 6d.

Entries to be Made in Mr. Trood's tent before
12 o'clock. To start at 2-45.

Starter—M. Stone, Esq.

Judge and Referee—C. Dickens, Esq.

Clerk of the Course—C. Dickens, Junr., Esq.

Stewards and Keepers of the Course—Messrs. A. H.
Layard, M.P., H. Chorley, J. Hulkes, and H. Dickens.

Between 2,000 and 3,000 people attended these sports, and there was not a single case of misconduct or damage to property. Writing to Mr. Forster next day, Dickens says, " The road between this and Chatham was like a fair all day, and surely it is a fine thing to get such perfect behaviour out of a reckless seaport town."

There is, it may be noted, a passage in *The Holly Tree*, where Dickens—perhaps unconsciously—in the person of " Boots " thus describes his own well-known partiality for all wholesome open-air games and sports, thus—" and he ran, and he cricketed, and he danced, and he acted, and he done it all equally beautiful."

A *fac-simile* letter from Charles Dickens to Mr. W. B. Rye, thanking him for a copy of his little book,

K

Gad's Hill Place,
Higham by Rochester, Kent.

Friday Third November 1865

Dear Sir

I beg you to accept my
cordial thanks for your curious "Visits
to Rochester" as I prepared about its
old corners with interest and wonder
when I was a very little child, few
people can find a greater charm in
that ancient city than I do.

Believe me

Yours faithfully and obliged,

Charles Dickens

W. B. Rye Esquire

FAC-SIMILE OF LETTER FROM CHARLES DICKENS TO MR. W. B RYE.

Visits to Rochester, and dated Gad's Hill Place, November 3rd, 1865, may not be out of place here. (See opposite.)

On the 9th August, 1870 (just two months after the death of Charles Dickens), the writer was in the upper room of the châlet at Gad's Hill Place ; and but for the screaming of the swifts as they now and again swept past in their mysterious flight, the silence of the place was absolutely unbroken. The quill pens used in writing the last pages of *Edwin Drood*, and stained with the author's favourite blue ink, were still lying on the table, and one could not but feel " the appalling vacancy in the room he had occupied so recently, where his chair and table seemed to wait for him." [1]

Over the way, however, the quiet of the place was invaded to some purpose, " herds of shabby vampires Jew and Christian, over-ran the house. The capital modern household furniture, etc., is on view." [2]

In the library Mr. Luke Fildes, the illustrator of *Edwin Drood*, was making a sketch in oils of the interior of the room, since published and known as " The Empty Chair."

In the yard were still to be seen evidences of the master's love of out-door games. A set of bowls, a set of croquet, some American carriage bells, and, reared against a large dog-kennel, was " Aunt Sally," sticks and all, in a box.

[1] *David Copperfield*, Chap. XXXVIII.
[2] *Dombey and Son*, Chap. LIX.

SWISS CHÂLET, FORMERLY AT GAD'S HILL PLACE.

"My room is up among the branches of the trees ; and the birds and the butterflies fly in and out, and the green branches shoot in at the open windows, and the lights and shadows of the clouds come and go with the rest of the company."—*Letter to American Friend.*

In another sort of box—a loose box in the stable—
was an extremely friendly grey pony. He was, I believe,
the only living thing belonging to the departed writer
then left on the premises. He immediately fixed my
attention as embodying at once, in his own person, *two*
of his master's well-known characters; for was he not
" Trotty Veck " by name, and " the Aged " by reason of
his years ? While I patted his neck over the half-door,
he was diligently searching my pockets for possible
dainties in the shape of biscuits or apples, as if quite
used to it ; but at the same time with an unmistakably
woe-begone expression of countenance, as if, with him,
too, " regrets were the natural property of grey hairs." [1]

" Trotty Veck " was sold to a Mr. Abrahams for
twenty guineas, and is probably (like the hypothetical
" Gray " alluded to by Mr. Weller, senr.) long since " up
the universal spout o' natur." [2]

It is infinitely more agreeable, however, to turn from the
week of the sale at Gad's Hill Place, and to remember the
favourite residence of Charles Dickens as it is now, for the
house and grounds, beautifully kept by its present owner,
bring back to our memory Bret Harte's noble lines—

> . . . . " let its fragrant story
> Blend with the breath that thrills
> With hop-vines, incense all the pensive glory
> That fills the Kentish hills."

---

[1] *Martin Chuzzlewit*, Chap. X.
[2] *Master Humphrey's Clock*, page 422, Original Edition.

CHAPTER XIV.

RETROSPECTIVE NOTES AND ELUCIDATIONS.

" For my own part, my occupation in my solitary pilgrimages was to recall every yard of the old road as I went along it, and to haunt the old spots, of which I never tired. I haunted them, as my memory had often done, and lingered among them as my younger thoughts had lingered when I was far away."

David Copperfield, Chap. XXII.

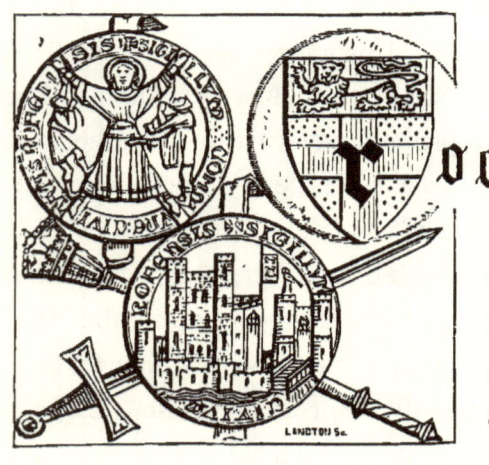

ochester and its Historic Picturesque surroundings, whether humourously described as " Mudfog," as " Dullborough," as " Our Town," or as " Cloisterham," will, as years roll on, become more and more closely associated with the life and work of Charles

Dickens ; and will, for all time to come, be acknowledged to have been "the birthplace of his fancy," his "boy hood's home !"

In the reminiscences of his early life, of which his books are full, we find, accordingly, many traces of his childhood at Chatham, many also of his struggling boyhood in London, and of his years of adolescence, remembrances not a few.

In these Notes and Elucidations very little criticism will be attempted, the object being, as before stated, to show how Dickens, throughout the whole course of his brilliant literary career, delighted to return to the scenes and recollections of his early boyhood.

Passing on, therefore, at once to his earliest printed pieces, the *Sketches by Boz, Illustrative of every-day Life and every-day People*, and taking them as they appear in the collected volumes, and not in the order in which they were written, we find in the second chapter of *Our Parish*, *The Old Lady*, who was the Mrs. Newnham, mentioned in Chapter IV. [*ante.*]

The row of houses there described is Ordnance Terrace, in which there are eleven houses, while in the *Sketch* the row is called Gordon Place, and the numbers run much higher than they do in the original. Gordon Place, it may be noted as a curious coincidence, is a short street out of Tavistock Square !

The Half-Pay Captain was also a resident of Ordnance

Terrace, and lived next door to the *Old Lady*, and his well-remembered oddity of behaviour was a constant source of amusement to the neighbours. "He is a charitable, open-hearted old fellow at bottom, after all ; so although he puts the *Old Lady* a little out occasionally, they agree very well in the main, and she laughs as much at each feat of his handiwork when it is all over, as anybody else."

In Chapter III., *The Four Sisters*, we are told, "The row of houses in which the *Old Lady* and her troublesome neighbour reside, comprises, beyond all doubt, a greater number of characters within its circumscribed limits, than all the rest of the parish put together."

This *Sketch* was written in 1834, and from a passage in it, telling us that the four sisters "settled in our parish *thirteen years ago*," we are taken back to the year 1821, when Dickens was living in Ordnance Terrace. There cannot, therefore, be a doubt that this, too, is some recollection of his boyhood.

The greater part of these *Sketches* contain reminiscences of more recent times, possibly, in the days when he was in Mr. Blackmore's employ.

Scotland Yard is situated within less than a quarter of a mile of the Blacking Works at Old Hungerford Stairs, and *The Sketch* is a graphic account of a curious district of London at that time (1823-4). "A few years hence and the antiquary of another generation, looking

EASTGATE, ROCHESTER.

into some mouldy record of the strife and passion that agitated the world in these times, may glance his eye over the pages we have just filled ; and not all his knowledge of the history of the past, not all his black-letter lore, or his skill in book collecting, not all the dry studies of a long life, or of the dusty volumes that have cost him a fortune, may help him to the whereabout, either of Scotland Yard, or of any one of the landmarks we have mentioned in describing it."

Seven Dials is wonderfully described : " Where is there such another maze of streets, courts, lanes, and alleys ? Where such a pure mixture of Englishmen and Irishmen as in this complicated part of London ? " This is true, to some extent, to the present day, as is also the curious account of the various articles of live and dead stock to be bought and sold there.

Here is a characteristic description of one of the dwellers in this strange locality : " The shabby-genteel man is an object of some mystery, but as he leads a life of seclusion, and never was known to buy anything beyond an occasional pen, except half-pints of coffee, penny loaves, and ha'porths of ink, his fellow-lodgers very naturally suppose him to be an author, and rumours are current in the Dials that he writes poems for Mr. Warren."

In *Doctors' Commons* are many glimpses of the London of Dickens' reporting days, and here as elsewhere in his works, so vivid, so truthful, are his descriptions of places and things now no longer in existence, that already the antiquaries of our day are taking a new and lively interest in Dickens, for the very love of his descriptions of these old times!

He gives here, in very few words, an account of a trial in the Arches Court, "the office of the Judge promoted by Bumple against Sludberry," which terminated in "the awful sentence of excommunication for a fortnight, and payment of the costs of suit" against Sludberry, "who was a little, red-faced, sly-looking ginger-beer seller," and who remarked "that if they'd be good enough to take off the costs, and excommunicate him for the term of his natural life instead, it would be much more convenient to him,——"

Through all these *Sketches* there runs a fine original vein of humour, set off here and there by a tender pathos which *all* can understand. Thus it came about that these *Sketches* were eagerly looked for long before the name of Charles Dickens was known, and even before he wrote under the name of Boz.

His first *Sketch* appeared in December 1833, and the first piece signed Boz was not published till August of the next year. It was the second chapter of *The Boarding House.*

Astley's and *Early Coaches* are juvenile experiences of his own, and he truly sketches himself as "a small boy of a pale aspect, with light hair,—coming up to town from school, under the protection of the guard, and directed to be left at the Cross Keys till called for."

Very interesting reading now is a *Parliamentary Sketch*, and in it we are taken back to the reporting days in the House of Commons, just after the great fire there, in October 1834, about which time this *Sketch* was undoubtedly written.

In Chap. XXII., *Gin-Shops*, a vivid picture of one of these glittering, brilliantly lighted saloons, is followed by a sentence or two worth thinking about. "Gin-drinking is a great vice in England, but wretchedness and dirt are a greater. If Temperance Societies would suggest an antidote against hunger, filth, and foul air, or could establish dispensaries for the gratuitous distribution of bottles of Lethe-water, gin-palaces would be numbered among the things that were."

In *A Christmas Dinner* and *The New Year* (1836) are some very striking reminiscences "of happy days and old times ;" in the latter *Sketch* we are introduced to Mr. Dobble, who was in a public office : "We know the fact by the cut of his coat, the tie of his neckcloth, and the self-satisfaction of his gait—the very green blinds themselves have a *Somerset House* air about them."

In *Shabby-Genteel People* are some very tender touches of description, as to what does and what does not entitle a man to be considered shabby-genteel.

" We will endeavour to explain our conception of the term which forms the title of this paper. If you meet a man, lounging up Drury Lane, or leaning with his back against a post in Long Acre, with his hands in the pockets of a pair of drab trousers plentifully besprinkled with grease-spots; the trousers made very full over the boots, and ornamented with two cords down the outside of each leg—wearing, also, what has been a brown coat with bright buttons, and a hat very much pinched up at the sides, cocked over his right eye—don't pity him. He is not shabby-genteel."

" We were once haunted by a shabby-genteel man; he was bodily present to our senses all day, and he was in our mind's eye all night. He first attracted our notice by sitting opposite to us in the *reading room of the British Museum;* and what made the man more remarkable was, that he always had before him a couple of shabby-genteel books."

In *Mr. Minns and his Cousin*, we find another *Somerset House* clerk, " or, as he said himself, he ' held a responsible situation under Government.'" The cousin was a Mr. Budden, which is a well-known name at Rochester. [See Gad's Hill.]

Of *The Tuggs's at Ramsgate*, it may be noted that in *Our Boys*, as acted, this *Sketch* is laid under contribution for a joke or two; here is one of them in exactly the same words. Mr. Tuggs (who dealt in Dorset butter) was asked by his new acquaintance, the captain, how he would go to Pegwell? " ' A shay ? ' suggested Mr. Joseph Tuggs. ' Chaise,' whispered Mr. Cymon. ' I should think *one* would be enough,' said Mr. Joseph Tuggs. ' However. two shays, if you like.' "

The notes on the *Sketches* may terminate with *The Great Winglebury Duel*, which abounds with recollections of Rochester, the description of the "long, straggling, quiet High Street, the small building with the big clock," etc., is unmistakable.

THE POSTHUMOUS PAPERS OF THE PICKWICK CLUB, known all the world over by the shorter title of *Pickwick*, are brim full of reminiscences of the writer's early life, from his boyish experiences at Chatham to his reporting days ! This is, on the whole, the most humourous of all his works, and still holds its place as the first favourite with the great bulk of the readers of Dickens.

Towards the middle of its publication it had attained a popularity that had probably never been equalled in the annals of fiction. It was about the time of the publication of the tenth part of the *Pickwick Papers* that the Rev. William Giles (for he had since the Chatham days been ordained as a Baptist minister) presented Charles Dickens with a silver snuffbox, in token of his admiration of the brilliant talents displayed by his old pupil. On the inside of the lid was his name, with a suitable inscription "to the Inimitable Boz," and the Inimitable he continued to be among his more intimate friends for the rest of his life.

In his *Letters* it will be seen that he was fond of playfully describing himself as "the inimitable," and it is probably a title which posterity will finally accept.

The origin of *Pickwick* is too well known to need recapitulation here, and it is only necessary to say that the scene opens in Goswell Street, London, and that Mr. Pickwick is at the outset driven to the Golden Cross Coach Office, to meet his friends, who are to take a journey with him into Kent, in search of adventures.

In the second chapter, the four Pickwickians take their seats on the Commodore Coach for Rochester, and Mr. Jingle joins them. Asked if he has any luggage, he replies, "Who—I ? Brown-paper parcel here, that's all, *other luggage gone by water,*— packing cases, nailed up,— big as houses,"—a clear reminiscence of the mode of carriage adopted by Mr. John Dickens when removing his heavier household goods from Chatham to London.

On reaching Rochester Bridge, and sighting the Castle, Jingle indulges in broken soliloquy till the coach stops at the Bull Hotel. Here the friends put up, and engage a private sitting-room.

The year 1827 (summer) is given as the date of this visit, and it may be remarked that the Bull Hotel is very little altered in appearance, inside or outside, since that

STAIRCASE AT THE BULL.

ORCHESTRA IN BALL-ROOM, AT THE BULL HOTEL.

time. The staircase shown in the engraving is now just as it was, with the addition, however, of a few more prints on the walls, and of the handsome hall-lamp from Gad's Hill Place. The ball-room, or assembly-room, where in times past many charity and county balls have been held, is just as it was in the *Pickwick* days.

" It was a long room, with crimson-covered benches, and wax-candles in glass chandeliers. The musicians were securely confined in an elevated den." . . . Mr. Hull's sketch is a capital representation of the entrance end of this room, and shows the little orchestra as it was and is to the present day.

It is rather difficult to realise, looking at this old room by the cold light of day, that " the Commissioner— head of the yard," and the no less important " Head of the Garrison (like two Alexander Selkirks, monarchs of all they surveyed) " should have met the Smithies, the Snipes, and the Tomlinsons of a bygone age, but it is quite true that (omitting the names) the wealth and fashion of the county of Kent have many a time been present at the grand balls formerly held in this hotel.

But on this particular occasion (the ball attended by Mr. Tupman and Jingle) an old acquaintance was present, and here is his portrait : he "was a little fat man, with a ring of upright black hair round his head, and an extensive bald plain on the top of it—Dr. Slammer, surgeon to the 97th. The doctor took snuff with everybody, laughed, danced, made jokes, played whist, did everything, and was everywhere."

The next day the unoffending Winkle accepted the challenge sent by the irate little doctor, and at sunset the combatants, with their seconds, met in the well-remembered fields at the back of Fort Pitt, the very place where the schools of Rochester and Chatham used to meet to settle their difficulties, and to contend in the more friendly rivalry of cricket!

"The whole population of Rochester and the adjoining towns rose from their beds at an early hour of the following morning, in a state of the utmost bustle and excitement. A grand review was to take place upon the Lines. The manœuvres of half-a-dozen regiments were to be inspected by the eagle eye of the commander-in-chief; temporary fortifications had been erected, the citadel was to be attacked and taken, and a mine was to be sprung." (Chap. III.)

Mr. Pickwick and his friends Winkle, Tupman, and Snodgrass,[1] were there, of course, and experienced the pleasure of waiting two hours in a front place, under

---

[1] With reference to this curious surname, it is perhaps something more than a coincidence, that there was formerly a Mr. Gabriel Snodgrass, an eminent shipbuilder at Chatham Dockyard, where he learned his business. For a full account of him, with his portrait, see *The European Magazine*, July 1799. He was resident at Chatham for many years, and would probably, almost certainly, be known to Charles Dickens when a boy, at least by repute.

ROCHESTER CASTLE FROM OLD BRIDGE.
(*After* DADSON.)

ROCHESTER BRIDGE AND CASTLE FROM FRINDSBURY.
(*After* DADSON.)

pressure of an unruly crowd behind them, and a military guard in front. Here the party make the acquaintance of Mr. Wardle, and are hospitably entertained, and afterwards invited to visit Manor Farm, Dingley Dell. On the morning of the next day, Mr. Pickwick "leant on the balustrades of Rochester Bridge (the old Bridge) contemplating Nature, and waiting for breakfast."

"On the left of the spectator lay the ruined wall, broken in many places, and in some overhanging the narrow beach below in rude and heavy masses: . . . Behind it rose the ancient castle, its towers roofless, and its massive walls crumbling away, but telling us proudly of its old might and strength. . . . On either side the banks of the Medway, covered with cornfields and pastures, with here and there a windmill or a distant church, stretched away as far as the eye could see, presenting a rich and varied landscape, rendered more beautiful by the changing shadows which passed swiftly across it, as the thin and half-formed clouds skimmed away in the light of the morning sun."

The view so happily described was precisely that shown in the engraving, from a drawing by the late William Dadson, and the other engraving on the same page, also after Dadson, assists the reader by showing an extended view of the valley of the Medway.

On consulting the waiter at breakfast, the friends are told, " Dingley—Dell—gentlemen—fifteen miles, gentlemen—cross road—post-chaise, sir?" Dingley Dell is of course wholly " in the air," but Muggleton?—"everybody whose genius has a topographical bent, knows perfectly well that Muggleton is a corporate town, with a mayor, burgesses, and freemen;—Mr. Pickwick stood in the principal street of this illustrious town, and gazed with an air of curiosity, not unmixed with interest, on the objects around him. There was an open square for the market-place ; and in the centre of it, a large inn with a sign-post in front, displaying an object very common in art, but rarely met with in Nature—to wit, a blue lion with three bow-legs in the air, balancing himself on the extreme point of the centre claw of his fourth foot."

Where, then, is Muggleton? Well—no one can say positively, but from the direction taken by the friends, as Mr. Winkle's horse went " drifting up the High Street," preceded by the chaise, I fancy they turned into the Maidstone Road out of Eastgate, past Restoration House, past the Blue-Bell, and through some of the most delightful country to be met with even in Kent, to Aylesford, and so over the bridge to West Malling or Town-Malling.

This place does not answer to much of the description, but I think it was in the mind of Dickens when he wrote the tale, the more so as it is certainly on a cross-road from Rochester, that the distance given by the

waiter is about right, and that when Wardle and Pickwick were chasing the runaway Jingle, they went by the
direct road from Malling to London, without coming
back through Rochester, which would have been a much
longer way.

One of the cricketers at Dingley Dell was Mr.
Struggles, which was the nickname of George Stroughill
(pronounced Stro'hill), the friend of Dickens when a boy
at Ordnance Terrace, Chatham!

The morning after the chase of Jingle and Miss
Wardle, Mr. Pickwick, Mr. Wardle, and Mr. Perker
enter the yard of the White Hart Inn in the Borough, and
introduce themselves at once to Sam Weller, who in his
turn a few days later on in the narrative, introduces his
father, Mr. Tony Weller, of the Marquis of Granby,
Dorking. A recent writer has tried to locate this hostelry
in one of the pleasant Surrey towns near London ; the
real origin, however, of the names of both the inn and its
master must be looked for at Chatham, where, in the old
Ordnance Terrace days, a Mr. Thomas[1] Weller kept the
Granby Head in the High Street !!

"On the opposite side of the road was a large sign-
board on a high post, representing the head and shoulders

[1] The transition from Tommy Weller to Tony Weller is not a very
violent one, and the origin of this celebrated character is obvious enough.
See also Mary Weller, in Chap. IV., *ante*—

Arn't that 'ere " Boz " a tip-top feller !
Lots writes well, but he writes Weller !
Tom Hood, in review of *Master Humphrey's Clock.*

of a gentleman with an apoplectic countenance, in a red coat, with deep blue facings, and a touch of the same blue over his three-cornered hat, for a sky, . . . and the whole formed an expressive and undoubted likeness of the Marquis of Granby of glorious memory."—*Pickwick Papers,* Chap. XXVII.

Having returned to Dingley Dell by the Muggleton heavy coach, Mr. Pickwick found that Mr. Tupman had gone away during his absence, but was to be heard of at "the Leather Bottle, Cobham, Kent, and the three friends at once resolve to follow him there." "At Muggleton they procured a conveyance to Rochester, where they had an early dinner, and having procured the necessary information relative to the road, the three friends set forward again in the afternoon to walk to Cobham."

" A delightful walk it was, for it was a pleasant afternoon in June, and their way lay through a deep and shady wood, cooled by the light wind which gently rustled the thick foliage, and enlivened by the songs of birds that perched upon the boughs. The ivy and the moss crept in thick clusters over the old trees, and the soft green turf overspread the ground like a silken mat."

(The friends were following the track of the Roman Watling Street, which runs almost in a straight line from Rochester to London, and a very considerable portion of which is still in existence as a country road.)

THE LEATHER BOTTLE, COBHAM, KENT.

"They emerged upon an open park, with an ancient Hall, displaying the quaint and picturesque architecture of Elizabeth's time. Long vistas of stately oaks and elm-trees appeared on every side, large herds of deer were cropping the fresh grass, and occasionally a startled hare scoured along the ground with the speed of the shadows thrown by the light clouds which swept across a sunny landscape like a passing breath of summer.

"'If this,' said Mr. Pickwick, looking about him, 'if this were the place to which all who are troubled with our friend's complaint came, I fancy their old attachment to this world would very soon return.'

"'I think so, too,' said Mr. Winkle.

"'And really,' added Mr. Pickwick, after half-an-hour's walking had brought them to the village, 'really, for a misanthrope's choice, this is one of the prettiest and most desirable places of residence I ever met with.'"

Having been directed to the Leather Bottle, the friends entered, and were at once shown into the parlour, "a long, low-roofed room, furnished with a large number of high-backed, leather-cushioned chairs, of fantastic shapes, and embellished with a great variety of old portraits and roughly coloured prints of some antiquity. At the upper end of the room was a table, with a white cloth upon it, well covered with a roast fowl, bacon, ale, and et ceteras ; and at the table sat Mr. Tupman, looking as unlike a man who had taken his leave of the world as possible."

As this old house is, within and without, exactly as it was fifty years ago, I have given correct views of the exterior, and of the parlour. The portraits in oil (quite a number of them) are still there, and, although the house has changed hands several times since the days of Pickwick, the furniture is the same.

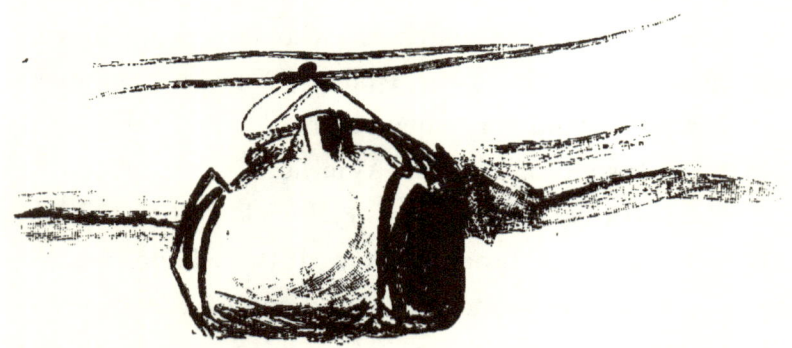

LEATHER BOTTLE FORMERLY USED AS THE SIGN.

At the time *Pickwick* was written, the veritable Leather Bottle shown here was to be seen attached to the sign over the door. It is still preserved in the bar.

It is worth noting that this description of Cobham, and its Leather Bottle, was undoubtedly written while Charles Dickens was staying at Chalk immediately after his marriage. He was at this time in lodgings, and his old landlord, Thomas White, is still living (1882).

Charles Dickens stayed a day and a night at the

PARLOUR OF THE LEATHER BOTTLE, COBHAM, KENT.

Leather Bottle with Mr. Forster in September 1841 (*vide* Forster's *Life*). That in his early days he stayed there on other occasions is certain, and in February 1845 Charles Dickens, Mrs. Dickens, Miss Hogarth, D. Maclise, Douglas Jerrold, and John Forster, visited Cobham Church and Park on a Sunday, their head-quarters being the Bull at Rochester.[1]

The fine old church of St. Mary Magdalen, Cobham, frequently alluded to by Dickens in his works, is shown here, from a careful drawing by Mr. Edward Hull.

The church is immediately in front of the Leather Bottle, and on the occasion of the visit of the four friends, Mr. Pickwick and Mr. Tupman withdrew to this quiet spot, and " for half an hour their forms might have been seen pacing the churchyard to and fro."

Charles Dickens was particularly fond of this delightful part of a delightful county, and his last walk, when his feet had well nigh " completed their journey," was on the evening of a beautiful summer day (the 7th June, 1870), when, with his sister-in-law,[2] he rambled through the shady lanes that surround Cobham Park.

Here is a fine description of the stillness and quiet to be found in a small village in the depths of the country at night. " It was past eleven o'clock—a late hour for

[1] The Leather Bottle was partially destroyed by fire on Good Friday, the 8th April, 1887.

[2] Miss Hogarth.

M

the little village of Cobham—when Mr. Pickwick retired to the bedroom which had been prepared for his reception. He threw open the lattice window, and setting his light upon the table, fell into a train of meditation on the hurried events of the two preceding days.

"The hour and the place were both favourable to contemplation ; Mr. Pickwick was roused by the church clock striking twelve. The first stroke of the hour sounded solemnly in his ear ; but when the bell ceased, the stillness seemed insupportable ;—he almost felt as if he had lost a companion."

On the morrow the friends walk on to Gravesend, a place frequently mentioned in the letters of Charles Dickens, and in several of his books, and where in later life he was often seen with his pony-chaise and dogs.

A few days after the discovery of the celebrated stone at Cobham, Mr. Pickwick has an adventure at Bury St. Edmunds, at a red-brick house called *Westgate House*, and which, like the now famous East Gate House at Rochester, was a ladies' school !

At the Magpie and Stump Mr. Pickwick makes the acquaintance of several lawyers' clerks, and some wonderful tales are told by old Jack Bamber of the " Inns," and the chambers therein, the " Queer Client " being, it would seem, his favourite. In it, at the opening of the tale, the High Street in the Borough, with the Marshalsea Prison, are introduced, and at the end

COBHAM CHURCH, KENT.

reference is made to "one of the most peaceful and secluded churchyards in Kent, where wild-flowers mingle with the grass, and the soft landscape around forms the fairest spot in the Garden of England." This is probably another allusion to Cobham, or it will answer equally well for the adjoining parish of Shorne, which was also a favourite locality with Dickens.

In this tale, Heyling, the "queer client," finds his enemy, a decrepit old man, living at Little College Street, in Old Pancras Road, the same street Charles Dickens had lodged in when a boy, and where the original of Mrs. Pipchin was then living!

On the breaking up of the Christmas party at Dingley Dell, Mr. Bob Sawyer invites Mr. Pickwick and friends to come and see him at his lodgings in Lant Street, in the Borough, where Dickens had also lived in his boyhood, and it is noteworthy that one of Bob's friends, Mr. Jack Hopkins, a medical student from St. Bartholomew's, was the namesake of one of the prominent characters in the prison scenes at the King's Bench given in *Copperfield*.

The visit to Bath and Bristol is probably a recollection of the reporting days; the *Bush*, at Bristol, was Dickens' Hotel at that time. (*Vide* Forster's *Life*.)

In the Fleet Prison one of the interesting party on whom Mr. Pickwick was "chummed" was a butcher of whom Mr. Roker remarks, " as he gazed abstractedly out of the grated window before him, as if he were fondly recalling some peaceful scene of his early youth ; it seems but yesterday that he whopped the coal-heaver down Fox-under-the-hill by the wharf there,"—the locality being that of the blacking manufactory, and the fight, probably enough, an actual occurrence.

Some of the most telling fun in all *Pickwick* is in Chap. XLV., where old Weller visits Sam in the Fleet, and the most pathetic part is that leading up to the death of the poor Chancery prisoner in the preceding chapter.

OLIVER TWIST is a standing protest against the atrocious poor-laws of a past generation. The hero of the tale, " a child of a noble nature and a warm heart," ' was a workhouse boy of unknown parentage, and in the opening of the story we are told that " Hunger and recent ill-usage are great assistants if you want to cry; and Oliver cried very naturally indeed."

In a letter to Rev. Thomas Robinson (April 8th, 1841), bearing on poor-law mal-administration, Dickens says, " I will pursue cruelty and oppression, the enemy of all God's creatures of all codes and creeds, so long as I have the energy of thought and the power of giving it utterance."

Again, in 1844, having just returned from Venice, he remarked to his friend and biographer, " Ah ! when I saw those places, how I thought that to leave one's hand upon

the time, lastingly upon the time, with one tender touch
for the mass of toiling people that nothing could
obliterate, would be to lift oneself above the dust of all
the Doges,"—and, says Forster, truly enough, " in varying forms this ambition was in all his life."—Forster,
vol. ii., page 122.

There is in this work some evidence of the influence
(it may have been an unconscious influence) exerted
upon him at this time by his friend William Harrison
Ainsworth ; it is less, perhaps, in the style of the writing, than in some of the more highly dramatic situations
of the plot. This feeling is, I think, heightened by the
fact that the illustrations to *Oliver* were designed and
etched by George Cruikshank, who at this time was in
the enjoyment of the full measure of his extraordinary
powers, and was, besides, engaged during its publication
in illustrating the works of Ainsworth.

Though none of the incidents of the tale can be said
to resemble points in the early life of the author, there
is yet a sufficient general resemblance in thought and
feeling between the imaginative hardly used Oliver and
his originator when a boy, to make it easy of recognition
to the student, or even to the ordinary careful reader of
the works of Dickens.

The sketch of Mr. Fang, the police magistrate, whose
eccentric outbursts of temper were continually bringing
him into unenviable notice, is a recollection of the

reporting days. In reading it we are reminded of a sally of Mr. Samuel Weller, where he says, "This is a very impartial country for justice. There ain't a magistrate going as don't commit himself twice as often as he commits other people."

It may perhaps interest readers to note the similarity in thought and style of the following two passages, one in *Oliver Twist*, Chap. V., where Oliver runs away from the undertaker Sowerberry, who has tried to show him that, however he disliked the business at first, he would in time get used to it, the other in *David Copperfield*, Chap. II.

"Oliver wondered, in his own mind, whether it had taken a very long time to get Mr. Sowerberry used to it. But he thought it better not to ask the question."

In *David Copperfield* (written in the first person) little David tells how there was a mural tablet in the church to the late Mr. Bodgers, whereon, among other things, it stated that "physicians were in vain," and, says David, "I wonder whether they called in Mr. Chillip, and he was in vain ; and if so, how he likes to be reminded of it once a week."

These two passages are fair specimens of the quaint, precocious thoughtfulness that Dickens has thrown into the utterances of many of his youthful characters !

MUDFOG ASSOCIATION, 1837-38. "Mudfog is a pleasant town—a remarkably pleasant town—situated in a charming hollow by the side of a river, from which river Mudfog derives an agreeable scent of pitch, tar, coals, and rope-yarn, a roving population in oil-skin hats, a pretty steady influx of drunken bargemen, and a great many other maritime advantages."

This is evidently a humorous description of Chatham, and it is more than probable that Rochester is included in the general satire.

Of the mayor, Mr. Nicholas Tulrumble, we are told that he began life as a coal-dealer, with a capital of two-and-ninepence.

" Time, which strews a man's head with silver, sometimes fills his pockets with gold." It was so with Nicholas Tulrumble, and it is recorded that he afterwards became mayor of Mudfog, and lived at Mudfog Hall, on Mudfog Hill.

It is curious to note that among the names of eminent men attending the meetings of the *Mudfog Association* was a Mr. Waghorn, a well-known and respected family name at Chatham, of which the late Lieutenant Waghorn was a member. Sowster is also an old Chatham name. " I have procured a local artist to make a faithful sketch of the tyrant Sowster (the Beadle of Mudfog). His whole air is rampant with cruelty, nor is the stomach less characteristic of his demoniac propensities."

The curious Inn signs mentioned in these papers, such as the Black-Boy-and-Stomach-ache, the Boot-Jack —and Countenance, and the Original-Pig, it might be difficult to find !

In NICHOLAS NICKLEBY the reader may get many glimpses of the early life of Dickens himself, and although it would be difficult to say which of the actual incidents of this great work are fact, and which fiction, in the full acceptation of the word, there can be no doubt that many of the experiences of Nicholas are recollections of the early associations of the author.

The tale opens with allusions to Devonshire, a county which he has mentioned in several other books. Towards the close of *Nicholas Nickleby* Charles Dickens went into Devonshire, and took and furnished Mile-end Cottage, Alphington, near Exeter, for his father and mother, as mentioned in a previous chapter. A very humorous account of his negotiations with the proprietor of this house is given in Mr. Forster's book, vol i., p. 163.

" I took a little house for them this morning (5th March, 1839, from the New-London Inn), and if they

are not pleased with it I shall be grievously disappointed.
Exactly a mile beyond the city, on the Plymouth Road,
there are two white cottages: one is theirs, and the
other belongs to their landlady. I almost forget the
number of rooms, but there is an excellent parlour, with
two other rooms, on the ground floor ; there is really a

MILE-END COTTAGE, NEAR EXETER.

beautiful little room over the parlour, which I am fur-
nishing as a drawing-room, and there is a splendid
garden."

The accompanying engraving of this cottage is from
a sketch kindly made by Mr. W. B. Rye, expressly for
this work, and with it the reader may compare a description of this same cottage, which is to be found in
Nicholas Nickleby, Part 2, Chap. XXIII., where it is

specially mentioned by Mrs. Nickleby as " the beautiful little thatched white house one storey high, covered all over with ivy and creeping plants, with an exquisite little porch with twining honeysuckles and all sorts of things."

In a letter to Mr. Mitton of about the same date, Dickens says of this white cottage, " I don't think I ever saw so cheerful or pleasant a spot." [1]

Of the places dear to him in his infancy, Dickens mentions in this book Portsmouth, where Nicholas and Smike performed at the theatre, under the management of Mr. Vincent Crummles. The description of the theatre and the company is as good as anything in the tale, and " a strong smell of orange-peel and lamp-oil, with an under-current of sawdust," may almost be perceived as we read Chapter XXII.

There are references, too, to some old places in London, well known to him in his boyhood, and in the Preface he says, " I cannot call to mind, now, how I came to hear about Yorkshire schools when I was a not very robust child, sitting in bye-places near Rochester Castle, with a head full of PARTRIDGE, STRAP, TOM PIPES, and SANCHO PANZA."

---

[1] At a property sale held in Exeter, March 30th, 1885, Lot 1 was thus described : "A house at Alphington, called Mile-end Cottage, at one time occupied by Charles Dickens, held for forty-seven years, unexpired, from the Right Hon. Earl of Devon, at £10 a year, and in a very dilapidated condition." Sold to Mr. Smith for £83.

In severe weather, early in 1838, Charles Dickens, and Hablot Knight Browne (Phiz), names which must be henceforward inseparably connected for all time, undertook a long journey by coach into the North of Yorkshire to see for themselves something of these Yorkshire schools.

One result of their joint work in pen and pencil has been the complete obliteration of these pestilent and " cruel habitations." Probably not a single example of this low type of schools remains to the present day.

MASTER HUMPHREY'S CLOCK, with its two continuous tales, and introductory chapters, cannot be said to contain many recollections of the early life of the author ; but there is probably in the story of Joe Toddy-high and his sad experience of " benefits forgot," some hidden reminiscence of his own boyish days. Master Humphrey also, when he says in an opening chapter, " I do not know whether all children are imbued with a quick perception of childish grace and beauty and a strong love for it, but I was," does but echo the well-known sentiments of his Creator !

In the Preface we are told how Master Humphrey and his friends would probably " trace some faint reflection of their past lives in the varying current of the tale." I have always thought that in the life of Little Nell, there is in some way such a reflection of his own life.

In Dick Swiveller and his friends, and in Sampson

Brass, and the Notary, there is, no doubt, a vivid sketch of persons Dickens had himself encountered in the days of the law.

In the OLD CURIOSITY SHOP, the characters introduced seem to be real living men and women, and of its heroine, Lord Jeffrey has well said, that there has been " nothing so good as Nell since Cordelia."

BARNABY RUDGE, being mainly a description of the riots of 1780, and therefore an historical tale, has no special allusions to the early days of the writer ; but there is in that fine thirty-third chapter commencing, " One wintry evening," etc., a most interesting recollection of his early reading of the works of Smollett. In *Peregrine Pickle*, Chap. II., the landlord of a public-house where Trunnion and his cronies met nightly, hears a voice in the distance hailing : " Ho ! the house ahoy !" on which he, " clapping a hand to each side of his head, with his thumbs fixed to his ears, rebellowed in the same tone Hilloah ! "

In *Barnaby Rudge* Dickens makes John Willet, on hearing the cry of " Maypole, ahoy !" " clap his two hands to his cheeks, and send forth a roar which made the glasses dance and rafters ring—a long, sustained, discordant bellow, that rolled onward with the wind," etc.

A CHRISTMAS CAROL (1843) opens with a Christmas Eve and a wonderful description of a London fog. Scrooge having dismissed his clerk for the night, the office was closed in a twinkling, and poor Bob Cratchit having gone down a slide " at the end of a lane of boys twenty times, in honour of its being Christmas Eve, ran home to *Camden Town* as hard as he could pelt to play at Blind-man's-buff."

On going home to his old-fashioned roomy City house, Scrooge is visited by the ghost of his deceased partner Marley, who introduces the spirits of Christmas past, of Christmas present, and of Christmas yet to come.

The spirit of Christmas past takes Scrooge by the hand, and they pass out into the open country, and, incredible as it may seem to those who know how different in every particular Charles Dickens was, to that curious creation of his own fancy, Scrooge, we yet find that in some particulars the childhood of Scrooge was the childhood of himself.

" ' Good heaven ! ' said Scrooge, clasping his hands together, as he looked about him, ' I was bred in this place ; I was a boy here ! '

' You recollect the way ? ' inquired the Spirit. ' Remember it ! ' cried Scrooge, with fervour, ' I could walk it blindfold.'

" They walked along the road, Scrooge recognising every gate, and post, and tree, until a market town appeared in the distance, with its bridge, its church, and winding river."—" They left the high-road by a well-remembered lane, and soon approached a mansion of dull red-brick, with a little weather-cock surmounted cupola on the roof, and a bell hanging in it."

This curious mixing up of the boyhood of Scrooge with his own, seems to have been something more than a passing fancy, for in a letter to Mr. W. H. Wills, dated Folkestone, September 16th, 1855, he writes thus :—

" My dear Wills,—Scrooge is delighted to find that Bob Cratchit is enjoying his holiday in such a delightful situation ; and he says (with that warmth of nature which has distinguished him since his conversion), ' Make the most of it, Bob ; make the most of it.' "

The purposely confused account of his old school near Clover Lane, with his later school, and the red brick house with the cupola (Gad's Hill Place), is at least remarkable. The reader will find, too, that Master Scrooge had a little sister Fanny, who came to fetch him home from school !

Further on in the tale the ghost of Christmas present takes Scrooge to his nephew's house, and we are told that " Scrooge's niece played well upon the harp ; and played among other tunes, a simple little air (a mere nothing,—you might learn to whistle it in two minutes) which had been familiar to the child who fetched Scrooge from the boarding-school—when this strain of music sounded, all the things that the ghost had shown him came upon his mind, he softened more and more."

In Stave Four the ghost of Christmas yet to come

conducts Scrooge to the house of Bob Cratchit at Camden Town (he had been there before with the second spirit), "through several streets familiar to his feet," and he sees Bob Cratchit surrounded by his children, save one, Tiny Tim, who is lying dead upstairs. Mrs. Cratchit and the girls are busy with the mourning, and the funeral is to take place on Sunday. Poor Bob has been to see the place where his child is to be buried, and Mrs. Cratchit says, " You went to-day, then, Robert ? "

" Yes, my dear," returned Bob ; " I wish you could have gone. It would have done you good to see how green a place it is. But you'll see it often. I promised him that I would walk there on a Sunday. My little, little child ! " cried Bob ; " my little child ! "

" He broke down all at once. He couldn't help it. If he could have helped it, he and his child would have been further apart, perhaps, than they were."

Thomas Hood, in a review of this matchless performance in the January number of *Hood's Magazine* for 1844, thus speaks of the *Christmas Carol :—*

" If Christmas, with its ancient and hospitable customs, its social and charitable observances, were in danger of decay, this is the book that would give them a new lease. The very name of the author predisposes one to the kindlier feelings ;—it was a blessed inspiration that put such a book into the head of Charles Dickens, a happy inspiration of the heart, that warms every page."

N

As there is very little that can be considered to be retrospective in the rest of the Christmas books, they may be taken *seriatim* here instead of in the strict order of time of publication.

THE CHIMES, written in Italy in 1844, and read from the proofs on Monday, December 2nd, to the illustrious company, represented in Daniel Maclise's celebrated sketch,[1] was avowedly "a great blow for the poor," but is not otherwise noticeable here. Of the eleven persons represented in the above-named sketch, not one now survives !

THE CRICKET ON THE HEARTH, 1845, and THE BATTLE OF LIFE, 1846, have no special interest for the purposes of this book. Written in the middle period of the working life of Dickens, they resemble some others of his works in this particular, that there is in them scarce a trace of the recollections of his own early life.

The original editions of these Christmas Books are now very valuable, and are specially sought for by collectors, on account of their choice illustrations by Maclise, Stanfield, Leech, Doyle, Tenniel, and Stone.

THE HAUNTED MAN, 1848. Besides the allusion to the death of his sister, quoted on page 17, *ante*, there is in this little book some recollection of the old College at Cobham. It is somewhat obscured with the encroachments "of the great city," but there can be little doubt

---

[1] Forster's *Life of Charles Dickens*, vol. ii.

as to the locality Charles Dickens had in his mind when he wrote the following lines : " The last glimmering of daylight died away from the ends of avenues ; and the trees, arching overhead, were sullen and black. When in parks and woods, the high wet fern and sodden moss and beds of fallen leaves and trunks of trees were lost to view, in masses of impenetrable shade. When lights in old halls and in cottage windows were a cheerful sight. When the mill stopped, the wheelwright and the black-smith shut their workshops, the turnpike-gate closed, the plough and harrow were left lonely in the fields, the labourer and team went home, and the striking of the church clock had a deeper sound than at noon, and the churchyard wicket would be swung no more that night."

He elsewhere describes the dwelling of the student as " an empty old pile of building, on a winter night, with the loud wind going by upon its journey of mystery—whence, or whither, no man knowing since the world began." . . .

MARTIN CHUZZLEWIT, 1843-4, is almost universally acknowledged to be one of the best, and most deservedly popular, of all the works of Charles Dickens. It abounds in descriptive passages of the highest order, and is in the great novelist's richest vein of humour. Written to illustrate the various kinds and degrees of selfishness, it introduces to the reader's notice some of the most interesting and curious of all the characters of Dickens.

The tale opens in the neighbourhood of Salisbury, and it will be noticed that Mark Tapley (a new development, and in some degree an improvement on Sam Weller) describes himself as "a Kentish man by birth." [1]

In Chap. V., while incidentally describing some of the shop windows Tom Pinch delighted to gaze at in the old city of Salisbury, he mentions a book shop " where children's books were sold, and where poor Robinson Crusoe stood alone in his might, with dog and hatchet, goat skin cap and fowling-pieces, calmly surveying Philip Quarll and the host of imitators round him, and calling Mr. Pinch to witness that he, of all the crowd, impressed one solitary foot-print on the shore of boyish memory, whereof the tread of generations should not stir the lightest grain of sand."

Farther on in this chapter (the evening service at the Cathedral being over), " Tom took the organ himself. It was then turning dark, and the yellow light that streamed in through the ancient windows in the choir was mingled with a murky red. As the grand tones resounded through the church, they seemed, to Tom, to find an echo in the depth of every ancient tomb, no less than in the deep mystery of his own heart. Great thoughts and hopes came crowding on his mind as the rich music rolled upon the air, and yet among them—something

---

[1] Tapley is one of the characters in Smollett's *Sir Launcelot Greaves*, where he is described as a Brewer.

more grave and solemn in their purpose, but the same—
were all the images of that day, down to its very lightest
recollection of childhood."

Chapter VII. introduces those amusing rascals
Montague Tigg and Chevy Slyme, the latter of whom is
detained at the Blue Dragon for an unpaid score,—"a
thing in itself essentially mean ; a low performance
on a slate, or possibly chalked upon the back of a
door."

Young Martin afterwards encounters Tigg at a pawnbroker's in London, where in a playful fashion he assists
him in pawning his watch, and farther on in the tale
(Chap. XXVII.), Tigg appears in " clothes of the newest
fashion and the costliest kind—precious chains and
jewels sparkled on his breast ; his fingers clogged with
brilliant rings,"—as chairman of the Anglo-Bengalee
Disinterested Loan and Life Assurance Company.

Tigg and his friend David, the pawnbroker's assistant
of former days, had " embarked in an enterprise of some
magnitude, in which they addressed the public in general
from the strong position of having everything to gain,
and nothing at all to lose."

To these impecunious scamps Jonas Chuzzlewit, a
sordid, ungainly man, was introduced, and took his seat
as a member of the board. There is, says Dickens, in
another place, " a simplicity of cunning no less than a
simplicity of innocence," and he then shows how Jonas

was thrown off his guard by the magnificence of Tigg and his surroundings. "It is too common with all of us, but it is especially in the nature of a mean mind, to be overawed by fine clothes and fine furniture.[1] They had a very decided effect on Jonas."

In Chap. XXXV. is a capital description of an old waterside inn, where Martin and Mark went on being set ashore, on their return from America; the descriptive sketch of this inn recalls to mind more than one old tavern still to be seen at Chatham.

"It had more corners in it than the brain of an obstinate man; was full of mad closets, into which nothing could be put that was not specially invented and made for that purpose; had mysterious shelvings and bulk-heads, and indications of staircases in the ceiling; and was elaborately provided with a bell that rung in the room itself, about two feet from the handle, and had no connection whatever with any other part of the establishment."

Of all descriptions of the now vanished coaching-days the ride from Salisbury to London in Chap. XXXVI. is surely the best. Dickens describes the coachman as doing things with his hat, "which nothing but an unlimited knowledge of horses and the wildest freedom of the road, could ever have made him perfect in.

[1] Rich clothes are oft by common sharpers worn,
And diamond rings felonious hands adorn.—*Martial.*

The guard, too! Seventy breezy miles a day were written in his very whiskers. His manners were a canter; his conversation a round trot. He was a fast coach upon a down-hill turnpike road; he was all pace. A waggon couldn't have moved slowly, with that guard and his key-bugle on the top of it."

As a slight test of the hold *Martin Chuzzlewit* has taken upon the public, it may be remarked, that, with perhaps the single exception of *Pickwick*, no work of fiction (by whomsoever written) contains so many characters whose names may be said to have " passed into the language!"

Bailey, jun., and Poll Sweedlepipe, Pecksniff, and Pinch, and Slyme, Sairey Gamp, and her mythical friend Mrs. Harris, Betsy Prig, Zephaniah Scadder, and Jefferson Brick, Mark Tapley, Tigg, and Todgers!

Writing to Mr. Forster when the work was in progress (November 2nd, 1843), Dickens says, "You know, as well as I, that I think *Chuzzlewit* in a hundred points immeasureably the best of my stories," And so, up to that time, it undoubtedly was.

DOMBEY AND SON, 1846-7-8. On the authority of Dickens himself (see Forster's *Life of Charles Dickens*, vol. ii., p. 327), much of the early part of this tale, so far as Paul Dombey is concerned, is in a manner autobiographical! From internal evidence alone, we might have been almost sure of this; for there is, in little

Paul, the same kind of quick, precocious intelligence, that we now know was so remarkable in little Charles Dickens.

Little Paul Dombey, however, in his early boyhood, knew nothing of the cheerful genial surroundings which had so much to do with the after life and fame of Charles Dickens ; and it is only when we come to the Pipchin days that we can see that Paul and his originator were identical.

" I hope you will like Mrs. Pipchin's establishment," wrote Dickens to Mr. Forster. " It is from the life, and I was there,—shall I leave you my life in MS. when I die ? There are some things in it that would touch you very much." This letter was written November 4th, 1846.

In Walter Gay, too, there is noticeable much of the prompt impulsive action and indomitable energy of Charles Dickens at his age ; and it is difficult to believe otherwise than that the author himself knew this well, and that his own youth was before his mind's eye when he makes Walter propose to Florence on the eve of their marriage, that they should go away on the morrow, and *stay in Kent* until their ship was ready for them at Gravesend.

Of the illustrations to *Dombey and Son*, it may be said that " Phiz " (Mr. Hablot K. Browne) was probably at his best during its publication, and many of these plates are amongst his finest efforts. " Browne is certainly interesting himself," says Dickens in a note to Mr. Forster, " and taking pains. I think the cover very good ; perhaps with a little too much in it, but that is an ungrateful objection." It must be owned, however, that a few of the earlier plates in *Dombey and Son* were not so happy, and Dickens said of one or two of them, that they were so " dreadfully bad " they made him " curl his legs up."

The objection was that the artist did not keep strictly to the text, and not that the illustrations were bad as works of art.

DAVID COPPERFIELD, 1849-50, is so obviously and transparently autobiographical, and has, moreover, been so frequently alluded to and quoted in the course of this work, that it cannot be necessary to do more than make a few brief comments on it here.

The tale opens at Blunderstone or Blundeston in Suffolk, six miles from Yarmouth, and farther on in the story, David is at school at Canterbury ; but it is certain that Dickens never was at Yarmouth till January 1849 (when he was thirty-seven years of age), and he probably never saw Canterbury in his boyhood at all. It is very likely, therefore, that but for an evident intention to obscure his own identity in this tale, Charles Dickens would have written Portsmouth instead of Yarmouth, and Rochester instead of Canterbury !

So, also, with some of the leading characters and incidents of the story, such as the brutal step-father Murdstone, the eccentric but practical aunt, Betsy Trotwood, with her odd companion, Mr. Dick.[1] Although these and others of the characters in *David Copperfield* are, if possible, more *real* than those of any other of the books of Charles Dickens, they have, perhaps, been introduced with the intention of making the autobiographical character of the work less easy of recognition.

In this tale, as in *Dombey and Son*, one of the greatest favourites of all the characters introduced is a seafaring man, or, as he styled himself, " a babby in the form of a great Sea Porkypine." Daniel Peggotty and Ned Cuttle are types of men still to be found in our seaport towns, and with such men, it is well known, Dickens was quite at home. It is perhaps worthy of notice, that Peggotty as a Christian name for a woman was, and is still, in use at Chatham, though many will think with Miss Betsy Trotwood, that it has a somewhat heathenish sound.

There is in Chap. XIII. an interesting account of David's flight from London, and his passing through Rochester, and sleeping by the side of a garrison gun, in one of the batteries just above his old house on the

---

[1] The name of this curious character was originally written " Mr. Robert," as may be seen on Folios 8 and 9 of the MS. at South Kensington.

Brook. Also a life-like sketch of "Old Charley," a drunken madman, who formerly dealt in second-hand clothes at Chatham.

Of Wilkins Micawber, "with that theer bald head of his," nothing new can be said, but that his genial loveable disposition is likely to be remembered for all time,— "in short—till something better turns up."

One other pleasant reminiscence of Dickens' own early days it is difficult to pass over. Who can doubt but that the light-hearted revels in the chambers in Gray's Inn, tenanted by Tommy Traddles, is nothing more than a recollection of the Furnival's Inn days so dear to himself? We are also told in this same chapter how Traddles (like Dickens himself, and like Walter Gay) "had taken his young wife down into *Kent* for a wedding trip."

The great secret of the success of *David Copperfield* is undoubtedly this, that not only has Charles Dickens, as it were, breathed into it the breath of his own life, but, as his friend Mr. Forster has beautifully said, " Childhood and youth live again for all of us in its marvellous boy-experiences." [1]

BLEAK HOUSE, 1852-3. Of the twelve alternative titles proposed for this book, see Forster's *Life of Charles Dickens*, vol. iii., page 31 ; *eight* of them commenced with Tom-all-alone's (see *ante*, page 60), as in the following

[1] *Life of Charles Dickens*, vol. iii., page 15.

examples :—Tom-all-alone's. The Solitary House that was always shut up. Tom-all-alone's. The Solitary House where the grass grew. Tom-all-alone's. The Solitary House where the wind howled.

All the trial titles are akin to these, and all suggest desolation and ruin, till at last the short but expressive *Bleak House* was adopted, and Tom-all-alone's, the curious place-name from the neighbourhood of Chatham, was only used incidentally in the tale, as the name of a dilapidated rookery in London.

Trooper George, Matthew Bagnet, and the " old girl," his wife, are life-like studies, if not actual reproductions of characters Dickens had known ; so are the numerous lawyers, and lawyers' clerks introduced in *Bleak House.*

It has occurred to me that the interior view of Chesney Wold in this story, showing the long drawing-room, was probably taken from Tabley Hall, Cheshire. The similarity is most striking.

In August 1881 I was at Tabley, and in conversation with the late Lord de Tabley I ventured to call his attention to the fact, and to ask him if it was possible that Hablot K. Browne could ever have seen this fine room. He replied, " It is possible enough, as Phiz and Dickens were in this neighbourhood together more than once." The reader will recollect that the owner of Chesney Wold was Sir *Leicester* Dedlock, and will perhaps agree with me that as Leicester is the old family

name of the De Tableys, here is another very remarkable coincidence !

THE SEVEN POOR TRAVELLERS. In the visitors'
book at Watts' Charity, Rochester, under date of May
11th, 1854, the following names may be seen :—

During this particular visit, Dickens was, no doubt,
studying the administration of the Charity at that time,
for use in the Christmas number of *Household Words.*
The introduction, describing, as it does, the internal
arrangements and surroundings of this probably unique
Charity, is in Dickens' best manner !

He had been wandering about the neighbouring
Cathedral, " and had seen the tomb of Richard Watts,
with the effigy of worthy Master Richard starting out
of it like a ship's figure-head." [1]

---

[1] See the engraving of this monument on page 81 (*Initial letter*).

The description of the building and accommodation for the travellers is, or was at that time, absolutely correct. Of the six little rooms set apart as dormitories

WATTS' CHARITY.

for the travellers, the account given by the matron in the tale is also quite accurate. "They sleep in two little outer galleries at the back, where their beds has always

been, ever since the Charity was founded. It being so
very ill-convenient to me as things is at present, the
gentlemen are going to take off a bit of the back-yard,
and make a slip of a room for 'em there, to sit in before
they go to bed.'

"'And then the six poor travellers,' said I, 'will be
entirely out of the house?'

"'Entirely out of the house,' assented the presence,
comfortably smoothing her hands. 'Which is considered
much better for all parties, and much more convenient.'

"I had been a little startled, in the Cathedral,
by the emphasis with which the effigy of Master
Richard Watts was bursting out of his tomb; but I
began to think, now, that it might be expected to come
across the High Street some stormy night, and make a
disturbance here."

An extract from the will of Richard Watts, retaining
the old spelling, may be interesting here. The will is
dated August 15th, 1579, and directs that to the almshouse already standing beside the Market Cross in the
City of Rochester, there be added "six severall rooms
with chimneys for the comfort placing and abiding of
the poor within the said Citte, and also to be made apt
and convenient places therein for VI. good Mattresses or
Flockbeds and other good and sufficient furniture to
harbor or lodge in Poor Travellers or Wayfare men being
no Common Rooges nor Proctors, and they the said

Wayfaring men to harbor and lodge therein no longer than one night unless sickness be the further cause thereof and those poor folks there dwelling shall keep the House sweete make the Beds see to the Furniture keep the same sweete and curtuorsly intreate the said Poor Travellers and to every of the said Poor Travellers at their first coming in to have IIIId. and they shall warm them at the fyre of the residence within the said house if nede bee."

The plain meaning of the testator, Richard Watts, is that six poor men should be courteously received and lodged for one night, and relieved with four-pence in money. The equally plain meaning of Charles Dickens was that the poor were *not* treated as Watts directs in his will, but were in fact pushed out of the house altogether, and had a slip of a room in the back-yard, where they could sit before going to bed.

This room is lighted, it may be added, by one ordinary street-lamp, ingeniously placed in the yard so that it shines alike into the room, and into the approach to the dormitories!

Rogues and tramping vagabonds swarm on the Kentish roads still, though the Proctors, as known to Watts, are extinct and forgotten; but it has always seemed to me that the good people of Rochester, instead of abolishing this Charity altogether, as was quietly

ROCHESTER CASTLE.
Showing Graveyard in the remains of Castle Moat.

O

proposed quite recently, ought rather to be proud of it, and after being quite sure they are relieving only the *deserving poor* (there are plenty of them), they should, in the common-sense interpretation of the Founder's Will, give to each " wayfare man " not only a bare four-pence of the present currency, but the relative equivalent of fourpence in 1579.[1]

Ample funds exist for doing this, as Watts, for the maintenance of this house, gave " to the Mayor and citizens, all other his lands, tenements, and estates for ever."

In this Christmas number for 1854, the strong love of Dickens for these old scenes of his boyhood must be apparent to all. His visit in the May of this year, when Mark Lemon was with him, must have been a great treat. Here is a brief description of the slumberous old city, written when Dickens was in the prime of life, and in the fullest enjoyment of his extraordinary powers :—

"The silent High Street of Rochester is full of gables with old beams and timbers carved into strange faces. It is oddly garnished with a queer old clock that projects over the pavement out of a grave red-brick building, as if time carried on business there and hung out his sign. Sooth to say, he did an active stroke of work in Rochester, in the days of the Romans, and the Saxons, and the Normans ; and down to the times of King John, when the rugged castle—I will not undertake to

[1] Fourpence in the time of Elizabeth would buy a poor man quite a little stock of provisions. What would it buy now ?

say how many hundreds of years old then—was abandoned to the centuries of weather which had so defaced the dark apertures in its walls that the ruin looks as if the rooks and daws had picked its eyes out."

The account of the treat to the poor Travellers on this occasion is of course wholly fictitious, although it is accepted as sober truth by many people both in Rochester and elsewhere.

After the genial author's imaginary company had been feasted with " turkey and a chine," and a jug of punch had been produced, they drank to the memory of good Master Richard Watts.

" It was the witching hour for story-telling. 'Our whole life, Travellers,' said I, ' is a story more or less intelligible, generally less ; but we shall read it by a clearer light when it is ended. I, for one, am so divided this night between fact and fiction, that I scarce know which is which.' "

The stories being finished, and the wassail too, the party broke up as the Cathedral bell struck Twelve.

" As I passed along the High Street I heard the waits at a distance, and struck off to find them. They were playing near one of the old gates of the city, at the corner of a wonderfully quaint row of red-brick tenements, which the clarionet obligingly informed me were inhabited by the minor canons. They had odd little porches over the doors, like sounding-boards over old

ROCHESTER CATHEDRAL AND CASTLE.

MINOR CANON ROW, ROCHESTER.
(See also *Edwin Drood.*)

pulpits, and I thought I should like to see one of the minor canons come out upon his top step and favour us with a little Christmas discourse about the poor scholars of Rochester, taking for his text the words of his Master relative to the devouring of widows' houses."

In the morning the party of the night before, after partaking of hot coffee and bread-and-butter, all came out into the street together, and there shook hands. " As for me, I was going to walk by Cobham Woods, as far upon my way to London as I fancied. And now the mists began to rise in the most beautiful manner, and the sun to shine ; and as I went on through the bracing air, seeing the hoar-frost sparkle everywhere, I felt as if all nature shared in the joy of the great birthday. By Cobham Hall, I came to the village, and the churchyard where the dead had been quietly buried, ' in the sure and certain hope ' which Christmas time inspired.—Thus Christmas begirt me, far and near, until I came to Black-heath, and had walked down the long vista of gnarled old trees in Greenwich Park, and was being steam-rattled through the mists, now closing in once more, towards the lights of London."

It may be well to close this note on the *Seven Poor Travellers* by giving the full inscription on the tablet to Richard Watts in the south transept of Rochester Cathedral :—

Sacred to the Memory
of RICHARD WATTS Esq:
a principal Benefactor to this City
who departed this life Sept. 10. 1579 at
his Mansion house on Bully hill called SATIS (so named
by Q. ELIZABETH of glorious memory), and lies
interr'd near this place as by his Will doth plainly
appear. By which Will dated Aug. 22. and proved Sep.
25. 1579. he founded an Almshouse for the relief of poor
people and for the reception of six poor Travelers
every night and for imploying the poor of this City.

The Mayor and Citizens of this City in
testimony of their Gratitude and his Merit
have erected this Monument A.D. 1736.
RICHARD WATTS Esq: then Mayor.

SIGNATURE OF RICHARD WATTS.

On another page an engraving of a fine memorial brass to Charles Dickens is given; it was very appro priately placed immediately under Watts' monument.

Though not strictly in chronological order, it will be convenient to take the rest of the Christmas stories here.

THE HOLLY TREE, 1855. There is a curious reminis cence in the opening of this tale, of the journey by

PRIORS' GATE, ROCHESTER.

coach to the "farther borders of Yorkshire," in the days before *Nickleby.*

When snowed up at *The Holly Tree* on a Yorkshire moor, the traveller having speedily exhausted the literature of the inn, amuses himself with recalling his experiences of inns, and a capital series of remembrances of nurse's stories, all connected with inns, follows.

" My first impressions of an Inn dated from the nursery ; consequently I went back to the nursery as a starting point, and found myself at the knee of a sallow woman with a fishy eye, an aquiline nose, and a green gown,[1] whose speciality was a dismal narrative of a landlord by the roadside, whose visitors unaccountably disappeared for many years, until it was discovered that the pursuit of his life had been to convert them into pies."

" Then there was the roadside Inn, renowned in my time in a sixpenny book with a folding plate, representing in a central compartment of oval form the portrait of Jonathan Bradford, and in four other compartments four incidents ·of the tragedy with which the name is associated,—coloured with a hand at once so free and economical, that the bloom of Jonathan's complexion passed without any pause into the breeches of the ostler, and, smearing itself off into the next division, became rum in a bottle."

[1] Evidently Mrs. Pipchin.

The Mitre Inn (previously mentioned) was next passed in review, and then " to be continued to-morrow," said I, " when I took my candle to go to bed."

But the bed took upon itself to continue the train of thought, and here Dickens alludes to the fact, mentioned in his *Life and Letters*, that he had for years dreamed of a dear friend (his young sister-in-law, Mary Hogarth) " sometimes as still living ; sometimes as returning from the world of shadows to comfort me ; always as being beautiful, placid, and happy, never with any approach to fear or distress." [1]

And so on, through a succession of inns in Switzerland, in France, in Wales, in the Highlands of Scotland, and in Cornwall, where there comes in a remembrance of a glorious excursion in which Dickens and Forster, and " Mac " and " Stanny " were in company, for the

---

[1] This frequently recurring dream or vision of Mary Hogarth (who died in 1837 "at the early age of seventeen "), through the whole of the rest of his life, is one of the most notable incidents in the career of Dickens ; and, if other evidence were wanting, might be instanced as a proof of the deeply affectionate nature of the man. It is remarkable that the words he wrote for her epitaph, "Young, beautiful, and good," are repeated (1838) in *Oliver Twist*, Chap. XXXIV., where, speaking of the illness of Rose Maylie, he says, " The young, the beautiful, and good ;" and again in Chap. XXXIX., also (1840) in *The Old Curiosity Shop*, at the death of little Nell, he says of her, " so young, so beautiful, so good." Finally, we have the same words in *Dombey and Son* (1847), Chap. L., where Walter Gay, speaking o Florence Dombey, says, " To think that she, so young, so good, and beautiful ! " This is surely not an involuntary reproduction of himself, but a studied, intentional, and very touching tribute to the memory of the dear young friend of his early days.

humorous account of which see Forster's *Life of Charles Dickens*, vol. ii., page 20.

In Dickens' account of the journey he says, " they made such sketches, those two men (Stanfield and Maclise), that you would have sworn we had the Spirit of Beauty with us as well as the Spirit of Fun."

THE WRECK OF THE GOLDEN MARY, 1856. Sixty-seven days out from Liverpool, the good ship *Golden Mary*, bound for California, strikes on an iceberg, and the crew and passengers having taken to the boats, the good qualities of the captain and mate at once become manifest.

The story opens with a capital description of two genial seamen, Captain Ravender and John Steadiman the mate. After a fine account of his ship, Captain Ravender describes his fellow-travellers :—

" Of my passengers, I need only particularise, just at present, a bright-eyed blooming young wife who was going out to join her husband in California, taking with her their only child, a little girl of three years old, whom he had never seen.—As the child had a quantity of shining fair hair, clustering in curls all about her face, and as her name was Lucy, Steadiman gave her the name of the Golden Lucy.[1]—So we had the Golden Lucy and the *Golden Mary*."

After thirteen days' exposure and privation in an open

[1] See *ante*, page 24.

boat the poor child dies and—"we buried the Golden
Lucy in the grave of the *Golden Mary.*"

THE PERILS OF CERTAIN ENGLISH PRISONERS, 1857.
The story is told by one Gill Davis, a private in the Royal
Marines, and the scene opens on board of the armed
sloop, *Christopher Columbus*, in the South American
waters off the Mosquito shore.

Of himself Gill Davis says : " I was a foundling child
picked up somewhere or another, and I always understood my Christian name to be Gill. It is true that I
was called Gills when employed at Snorridge Bottom,
betwixt Chatham and Maidstone, to frighten birds,—
but that had nothing to do with the baptism wherein I
was made, etc., and wherein a number of things were
promised for me by somebody, who let me alone ever
afterwards as to performing of them, and who, I consider, must have been the beadle. Such name of Gills
was entirely owing to my cheeks, or gills, which at that
time of my life were of a raspy description.

" In those climates you don't want to do much. I
was doing nothing. I was thinking of the shepherd
(my father, I wonder?) on the hill-sides by Snorridge
Bottom, with a long staff, and with a rough white coat
in all weathers all the year round, who used to let me lie
in a corner of his hut by night, and who used to let me
go about with him and his sheep by day when I could
get nothing else to do, and who used to give me so little

of his victuals and so much of his staff, that I ran away from him—which was what he wanted all along, I expect—to be knocked about the world in preference to Snorridge Bottom."

This is not the only local allusion in the tale; there is also mentioned a Mr. Commissioner Pordage, an old and esteemed name at Rochester. (See also the notes on *Little Dorrit.*)

In the portion of THE HAUNTED HOUSE, 1859, written by Dickens, are allusions to his own habit of work, to his belief or otherwise in ghosts in general, to his bloodhound Turk, and to his friend and solicitor, the late Fred Ouvry, Esq., who, as *Mr. Undery*, he describes as playing "whist better than the whole Law List, from the red cover at the beginning to the red cover at the end."

In the GHOST IN MASTER B.'s ROOM are apparently some playful reminiscences of past days: " Where is my little sister ? " said the ghost, " and where is the boy I went to school with ? "

" I entreated the phantom to be comforted, and above all things to take heart respecting the loss of the boy he went to school with. I represented to him that probably that boy never did, within human experience, come out well, when discovered. I urged that I myself had, in later life, turned up several boys whom I went to school with, and none of them had at all answered."

HARD TIMES, 1854. Published originally in *House-*

hold Words. . The argument of this tale, as explained by Dickens himself, is this: "My satire is against those who see figures and averages, and nothing else—the representation of the wickedest and most enormous vice of this time; the men who, through long years to come, will do more to damage the really useful truths of political economy than I could do (if I tried) in my whole life."

Coketown in this story is supposed to stand for Manchester, or some other of our Lancashire manufacturing towns. Of Josiah Bounderby (see also page 79 *ante*) it may be said that though he is undoubtedly to be met with occasionally in "the dark, and true, and tender north," he is also to be heard of sometimes in other parts of the world.

One of the least successful attempts in this or any of the books of Charles Dickens, is his rendering of the Lancashire dialect; the utterances put into the mouths of Stephen Blackpool, and others, in *Hard Times*, are very far from being correct.

By far the best, most spirited, and life-like part of this story is the description of Mr. Sleary and his circus riders, and it is interesting to note that the inscription on the sign of the Pegasus Arms, where the circus company put up,

> " Good malt makes good beer.
> Walk in, you'll find it here," etc., etc.,

was taken from an old Inn sign, *The Malt Shovel*, at the foot of Chatham Hill![1]

LITTLE DORRIT, 1855-6-7. The name Dorrit, with a slight alteration in the spelling, is taken from a Rochester family, and it is an interesting fact that in the graveyard of Rochester Cathedral are still to be seen two tombstones, side by side, on which are engraved the now historic names of Fanny Dorrett and Caleb Pordage!!

There are in this tale other curious revelations, which could not be coincidences merely, but must have occurred to the mind of the writer as recollections of his own boyhood Such are the prison experiences of the Dorrits.

Rochester is also incidentally mentioned with other places "on the Dover Road" in Book 2, Chap. XVIII.

A TALE OF TWO CITIES, 1859, is for the purposes of this book chiefly remarkable for a very graphic account of a journey at night on the Dover Road, in the old coaching days of 1775.

At the trial of Darnay, it was shown that on the journey to Dover he had "travelled back some dozen miles or more, to *a garrison and dockyard*, and there collected information ; a witness was called to identify him as having been, at the precise time required, in the coffee-room of an hotel in that garrison-and-dockyard town waiting for another person." The reference is to Chatham.

[1] Recently removed.

P

There is also a fine description of the neighbourhood of Soho Square, another of the residences of Dickens when a youth of seventeen or eighteen.

THE UNCOMMERCIAL TRAVELLER. In this series of papers (1860) the writer makes many allusions to memories of his early days, and well-known well-remembered places. To begin with, there is a telling description of the East End of London, familiar to Dickens from his early boyhood. In the article *Wapping Workhouse,* he describes his journey through the town, past the India House, with its memories of another Charles (Charles Lamb), pats his little wooden midshipman affectionately "on one leg of his knee-shorts for old acquaintance' sake," and so past Aldgate Pump, and Whitechapel Church, and finds himself " rather inappropriately for an Uncommercial Traveller—in the Commercial Road."

TRAVELLING ABROAD. The whole of these Uncommercial papers appeared in *All the Year Round,* and were written at a period of the author's life when he had come back, as it were, to live in the old neighbourhood ; hence the frequent references to well-remembered localities in Kent. Here is a delightfully fresh description of the Dover Road. " So smooth was the old high road, and so fresh were the horses, and so fast went I, that it was midway between Gravesend and Rochester, and the widening river was bearing the ships, white sailed or black-smoked, out to sea, when I noticed by the wayside a very queer small boy.

" ' Holloa ! ' said I, to the very queer small boy, ' where do you live ? '

" ' At Chatham,' says he.

" ' What do you do there ? ' says I.

" ' I go to school,' says he.

" I took him up in a moment, and we went on. Presently the very queer small boy says, ' This is Gad's Hill we are coming to, where Falstaff went out to rob those travellers, and ran away.'

" ' You know something about Falstaff, eh ? ' said I.

" ' All about him,' said the very queer small boy. ' I am old (I am nine), and I read all sorts of books. But *do* let us stop at the top of the hill, and look at the house there, if you please ! ! '

" ' You admire that house ? ' said I.

" ' Bless you, sir,' said the very queer small boy, ' when I was not more than half as old as nine, it used to be a treat for me to be brought to look at it. And ever since I can recollect, my father, seeing me so fond of it, has often said to me, " If you were to be very persevering and were to work hard, you might some day come to live in it ! " Though that's impossible ! ' said the very queer small boy, drawing a long breath, and now staring at the house out of window with all his might.

" I was rather amazed to be told this by the very queer small boy; for that house happens to be *my* house; and I have reason to believe that what he said was true."

The paper is a recollection of foreign travel, and represents the author as "looking out of the German chariot window in that delicious travellers' trance which knows no cares, no yesterdays, no to-morrows, nothing but the passing objects and the passing scents and sounds ! "

The infinite pity and compassion of Charles Dickens is nowhere better shown than in THE GREAT TASMANIA'S CARGO. " I travel constantly, up and down a certain line of railway that has a terminus in London. It is the railway for a large military depôt,[1] and for other large barracks. To the best of my belief, I have never been on that railway by daylight, without seeing some hand-cuffed deserters in the train." The subject of this paper is, however, an account of the condition of some of the survivors of the campaign in India after the Indian Mutiny, and landed from the troopship *Great Tasmania* at Liverpool.

The chapter on TRAMPS has some very shrewd and discriminating remarks as to the habits of these wanderers. Perhaps nowhere in England are greater numbers and greater varieties of the genus tramp to be encountered, than on the Dover Road. His description

[1] Chatham.

of the tramp's manner of sitting by the roadside with his legs in a dry ditch, or of sleeping in the sun lying on the broad of his back, is only equalled by his account of the grades and conditions of this far too numerous fraternity.

" He (the tramp) generally represents himself, in a vague way, as looking out for a job of work ; but he never did work, he never does, and he never will." Then there is the slinking tramp, the well-spoken, glib young man, the exemplary Mr. and Mrs. Anderson, who appear to have spent " the last of their little all on soap," they are so clean.

" But the most vicious, by far, of all the idle tramps, is the tramp who pretends to have been a gentleman,— this pitiless rascal blights the summer road as he maunders on between the luxuriant hedges, where (to my thinking) even the wild convolvulus and rose and sweet-briar are the worse for his going by, and need time to recover from the taint of him in the air."

Other sorts of tramps—the handicraft tramps who are to be found everywhere are then described. " Surely a pleasant thing if we were in that condition of life (knife grinding) to grind our way through Kent, Sussex, and Surrey. Clock mending, again, except for the slight inconvenience of carrying a clock under one arm, and the monotony of making the bell go,—what a pleasant privilege to give voice to the dumb cottage clock, and set it talking to the cottage family again." Dickens then fancies himself as a travelling clock-maker, getting a job to repair the turret stable clock at the Hall (Cobham Hall). "Our task at length accomplished, we should be taken into an enormous servants' hall, and there regaled with beef and bread and powerful ale. Then paid freely we should be at liberty to go, and should be told by a pointing helper to keep round over yinder by the blasted ash, and so straight through the woods, till we should see the town lights right afore us. So should we lie that night at the ancient sign of the Crispin and Crispanus (at Strood), and rise early next morning to be betimes on tramp again."

The tramping bricklayers and their ways, the tramping soldier, " his legs well chafed by his trousers of baize," the tramping sailor and others are next taken, and the paper closes with a vivid description of a famous camping ground near Gad's Hill, for which see the chapter on Gad's Hill.

DULLBOROUGH TOWN, " my boyhood's home, is of course Rochester, and in this paper are some of the best of the many glimpses given in the writings of Dickens of his own childhood in this place. The half-humorous, half-regretful mood in which this Chapter XII. is written is very noticeable, and it is more than probable that nearly all these incidents (recalled to the mind of Charles Dickens by a leisurely stroll through Chatham and

THE OLD BRIDGE, ROCHESTER.

(*After* DADSON.)

Rochester in the period of middle life) are literally his own experiences when a boy.

On leaving the Chatham station, which is here purposely confounded with the terminus of the S. E. R. at Strood, the first discovery is that "the station had swallowed up the playing-field." This playing-field was immediately in front of Ordnance Terrace, and the writer, among others, can speak to the perfect accuracy of this description, for it was at one time his playing-field, too !

" It was gone. The two beautiful hawthorn trees, the hedge, the turf, and all those buttercups and daisies, had given place to the stoniest of jolting roads ; while beyond the station an ugly dark monster of a tunnel kept its jaws open, as if it had swallowed them and were ravenous for more destruction.

" When I had been let out at the platform door, like a prisoner whom his turnkey grudgingly released, I looked in again over the low wall, at the scene of departed glories. Here, in the hay-making time, had I been delivered from the dungeons of Seringapatam, an immense pile (of haycock), by my countrymen, the victorious British (boy next door and his two cousins), and had been recognised with ecstasy by my affianced one (Miss Green), who had come all the way from England (second house in the terrace)[1] to ransom me

[1] No. 2, Ordnance Terrace, Chatham, which is close at hand.

and marry me." He then describes the scene of many a cricket-match between the rival schools of Boles's and Coles's (otherwise Baker's and Giles's), and turning away for a ramble through the town, finds that the old coach office of Timpson's is gone. "When I departed from Dullborough in the strawy arms of Timpson's *Blue-eyed Maid*, Timpson's was a moderate-sized coach-office," he then gives an exact description of what *S*impson's coach-office used to be in the memory of the middle-aged inhabitants of Rochester.

"Of course the town had shrunk fearfully since I was a child there. I found the High Street little better than a lane. There was a public clock in it which I had supposed to be the finest clock in the world : whereas it now turned out to be as inexpressive, moon-faced, and weak a clock as ever I saw.

" The Theatre[1] was in existence, I found ; and I resolved to comfort my mind by going to look at it. Richard the Third, in a very uncomfortable cloak, had first appeared to me there, and had made my heart leap with terror by backing up against the stage-box in which I was posted, while struggling for life against the virtuous Richmond.

" It was within those walls that I had learnt, as from a page of English history, how that wicked king slept in war time on a sofa much too short for him, and how fearfully his conscience troubled his boots."

[1] The Theatre Royal, Star Hill, Rochester.

GATEHOUSE AND CATHEDRAL PRECINCTS, ROCHESTER.
This Drawing was left unfinished at the death of the Artist, Mr. WILLIAM HULL.

Then follows an account of the way in which evil days had fallen upon this theatre, how part of it had been let to a dealer in wine and bottled beer, how it was as a theatre To Let, and hopelessly so, and how there had been no performance there, except of a panorama, for a long time. " No, there was no comfort in the Theatre. It was mysteriously gone, like my own youth. Unlike my own youth, it might be coming back some day, but there was little promise of it." The Theatre, new-fronted and entirely altered, is now (1885) turned into a Conservative Club !

The uncommercial spirits do not appear to have been improved by a visit to the Mechanics' Institution, nor the Corn Exchange, nor by wandering through the streets, recognising here and there a once familiar face. One such recognition it would be unpardonable to omit.

" I had not gone fifty paces along the street when I was suddenly brought up by the sight of a man who got out of a little phaeton at the doctor's door, and went into the doctor's house. Immediately the air was filled with the scent of trodden grass, and the perspective of years opened, and at the end of it was a little likeness of this man keeping a wicket, and I said, ' God bless my soul ! Joe Specks.'

" Through many changes and much work, I had preserved a tenderness for the memory of Joe, forasmuch as we had made the acquaintance of *Roderick Random* together, and had believed him to be no ruffian, but an ingenuous and engaging hero."

The Uncommercial Traveller makes himself known to Joe Specks who had married Lucy Green, and when their youngest child came in after dinner,—

" I saw again in that little daughter, the little face of the hayfield, unchanged, and it quite touched my foolish heart. We talked immensely, Specks and Mrs. Specks, and I, and we spoke of our old selves as though our old selves were dead and gone, and indeed, indeed they were —dead and gone as the playing field that had become a wilderness of rusty iron, and the property of S. E. R.

" When I went to catch my train at night I was in a more charitable mood with Dullborough than I had been all day ; and yet in my heart I had loved it all day too. Ah ! who was I that I should quarrel with the town for being changed to me, when I myself had come back so changed to it ! All my early readings and early imaginations dated from this place, and I took them away so full of innocent construction and guileless belief, and I brought them back so worn and torn, so much the wiser and so much the worse ! "

In *Night Walks* are some striking *Night Thoughts*,[1]

---

[1] It may be objected that surely there is nothing in the writings of Charles Dickens bearing any analogy to those of Dr. Edward Young ; but indeed there is, and here is a line from *Martin Chuzzlewit*, Chap. XLVII., that might have been taken direct from the *Night Thoughts*— " What words can paint tremendous truths like these ! "

suggested by the localities through which he wandered, and short as the paper is, there are in it some of the most characteristic descriptive passages, written in Dickens' best manner.

In his wanderings he haunts St. Sepulchre's, the Old Bailey, the King's Bench Prison, the Old Kent Road, and so round by Bethlehem Hospital, to Westminster, and Old Palace Yard. Westminster Abbey suggested "a wonderful procession of its dead among the dark arches and pillars, each century more amazed by the century following it than by all the centuries going before."

The chapter on *Chambers* opens thus: "Having occasion to transact some business with a solicitor who occupies a highly suicidal set of chambers in *Gray's Inn*, I afterwards took a turn in the large square of that stronghold of melancholy, reviewing with congenial surroundings my experiences of chambers."

He then describes various chambers in the different Inns, and first we have a description of a set of chambers reminding us of those of Tommy Traddles in *Copperfield*, for he tells us of "a young fellow who had sisters, and young country friends, and who gave them a little party—in the course of which they played at Blindman's Buff." [1]

In one set of chambers a mysterious visitor walks in

---

[1] See also page 187, for another mention of these chambers.

at night, and claims all the furniture as his, and, upon a decanter of gin being produced, with sugar and hot water to assist, " the visitor drank the whole before he had been an hour in the chambers by the chimes of the church of St. Mary in the Strand."

The NURSE'S STORIES resemble strongly in their daring improbability, and quaint humour, some of the stories told by Mr. W. R. S. Ralston, and notably some of his *Russian Folk Tales.*

Whether we are indebted to Mrs. Pipchin for some of these " hair-raising nightmares " cannot now be known. It is certain, however, that some of the uncanniest of them all had their origin, or were suggested, in the Ordnance Terrace days at Chatham, and it is equally certain that Mary Weller was the young woman who told some of these ' *Stories.*'

" The first diabolical character who intruded himself on my peaceful youth (as I called to mind that day at Dullborough) was a certain Captain Murderer. This wretch must have been an offshoot of the Blue-Beard family, but I had no suspicion of the consanguinity in those times.—The young woman who brought me acquainted with Captain Murderer had a fiendish enjoyment of my terrors, and used to begin, I remember— as a sort of introductory overture—by clawing the air with both hands, and uttering a long low hollow groan.

" So acutely did I suffer from this ceremony in combination with this infernal captain, that I sometimes used to plead I thought I was hardly strong enough and old enough to hear the story again just yet. But she never spared me one word of it.—This female bard—may she have been repaid my debt of obligation to her in the matter of nightmares and perspirations !—reappears in my memory as the daughter of a shipwright. Her name was Mercy, though she had none on me."

There is a strong flavour of shipbuilding in the story of a shipwright whose name was Chips, who worked in the Government Yard ; " his father's name before him was Chips, and *his* father's name before *him* was Chips, and they were all Chipses."

While Chips was working in the Yard on some repairs to an old Seventy-four, the Devil appeared to him, and ultimately Chips sold himself to the Evil One (" the bargain had run in the family for a long time ") for " an iron pot and a bushel of tenpenny nails, and half a ton of copper, and a rat that could speak."

This rat was a *thought-reading* animal, and sometimes not only anticipated the utterances of Chips, but came out with the following refrain in reply—

> A Lemon has pips,
> And a Yard has ships,
> And *I'll* have Chips.

Those who knew Charles Dickens personally, will

Q

remember well the delight he took in such gruesome tales as these *Nurse's Stories.*

In BIRTHDAY CELEBRATIONS, mentioned in a former chapter, are to be found unmistakable recollections of his own happy childhood.

" My memory presents a birthday when Olympia and I were taken by an unfeeling relative—some cruel uncle, or the like—to a slow torture called an Orrery. The terrible instrument was set up at the local Theatre, and I had expressed a profane wish in the morning that it was a play ; for which a serious aunt had probed my conscience deep, and my pocket deeper, by reclaiming a bestowed half-crown."

'" The first magic lantern I ever saw was secretly and elaborately planned to be the great effect of a very juvenile birthday ; but it wouldn't act, and its images were dim. My experience of adult birthday magic lanterns may possibly have been unfortunate, but has certainly been similar."

And so, through a variety of birthdays up to manhood, the paper ending with a humorous description of an imaginary celebration of Shakespeare's Birthday at Dullborough.

CHATHAM DOCKYARD, 1860. In this chapter we are taken to the marshy country on the banks of the estuary of the Thames, near Cooling ; a delightfully quiet place for an idle ramble on a fine summer day, and a part of the country that Dickens first became acquainted with on his taking up his residence at Gad's Hill Place, distant six or seven miles. He was afterwards, to the close of his life, very partial to these low-lying marshes, and made use of them again in 1861, in *Great Expectations.*

This curious corner of the county of Kent has quite recently been made accessible to all, by a new branch line of the South-Eastern Railway, and is well worth a visit. Only by a personal visit on a suitable day can the freshness and accuracy of the descriptive parts of this Chapter, and of those in *Great Expectations,* be fully realised and appreciated.

Near an old fort in these marshes the *Uncommercial Traveller* meets a boy "with an intelligent face burnt to a dust colour by the summer sun, and with crisp hair of the same hue. He is a boy in whom I have perceived nothing incompatible with habits of studious inquiry and meditation, unless an evanescent black eye (I was delicate of inquiring how occasioned) should be so considered."

With this boy "I recently consorted on a breezy day when the river leaped about us, and was full of life.—Peace and abundance were on the country side in beautiful forms and beautiful colours, and the harvest seemed even to be sailing out to grace the never-reaped sea in the yellow-laden barges that mellowed the distance.—While he (the boy) thus discoursed, he several times directed his eyes to one distant quarter of the landscape, and spoke with vague mysterious awe of 'the Yard.' Pondering his lessons after we had parted, I bethought me that the Yard was one of our large public Dockyards, and that it lay hidden among the crops down in the dip beyond the windmills, as if it modestly kept itself out of view in peaceful times, and sought to trouble no man. Taken with this modesty on the part of the Yard, I resolved to improve the Yard's acquaintance."

Accordingly he takes boat and crosses the Medway, and landing at the stairs, proceeds to examine and describe the gun-wharf, the building of the *Achilles*, with his twelve hundred clattering and banging workmen, the tributary workshops, where they make rivets, punch holes in the iron plates, and shear off superfluous portions of thick iron ; where they make oars for the ships' boats, and saw timbers for the ships. After this he comes to the sauntering part of his expedition, and consequently to the core of his uncommercial pursuits.

" Everywhere, as I saunter up and down the Yard, I meet with tokens of its quiet and retiring character. The white stones of the pavement present no other trace of *Achilles* and his twelve hundred banging men (not one of whom strikes an attitude) than a few occasional echoes. But for a whisper in the air suggestive of saw-dust and shavings, the oar-making and the saws of many movements might be miles away. Down below here is the great reservoir of water where timber is steeped in various temperatures, as a part of its seasoning process. Above it, on a tram-road supported by pillars, is a Chinese Enchanter's Car, which fishes the logs up, when sufficiently steeped, and rolls smoothly away with them to stack them. When I was a child (the Yard being then familiar to me) I used to think that I should like to play at Chinese Enchanter, and to have that apparatus placed at my disposal by a beneficent country.

Sauntering among the rope-making, I am spun into a state of blissful indolence, wherein my rope of life seems to be so untwisted by the process as that I can see back to very early days indeed."

In TITBULL'S ALMSHOUSES occurs again a distinct reference to the venerable College at Cobham : " A charming rustic retreat for old men and women ; in a quaint ancient foundation in a pleasant English county, behind a picturesque church and among rich old convent gardens."

With the MEDICINE MEN OF CIVILISATION, in which are some well-considered strictures on the follies of our modern Funeral customs, and a reminiscence of a funeral which he attended when a very little boy, these *Uncommercial Notes* must terminate. The Chapters of the *Uncommercial Traveller*, written in the prime of the author's life, and exhibiting as they do very favourably his unrivalled descriptive powers, may yet be said to be tinctured with sadness; but Charles Dickens has left it on record (*Nicholas Nickleby*, Chap. VI.) that, "memory, however sad, is the best and purest link between this world and a better!"

The story of GREAT EXPECTATIONS, 1861, appeared originally in *All the Year Round.* It may be observed that upon Charles Dickens purchasing Gad's Hill Place, and going to reside there, his old love for the neighbourhood seems at once to have revived; not that it had ever really relaxed at any period of his life, but from that time, the favourite localities of his boyhood again appear prominently in his works.

In the first chapter little Pip, the hero of the tale, is introduced, and in Cooling Churchyard, shown in the engraving, a convict escaped from the hulks at Chatham suddenly pounces on him, and under threats of having "his heart and his liver," makes him promise to bring him in the morning a file, and some "wittles."

A fine account follows of the morning mists on the marshes, in the depths of winter; and the humour turns to pathos in the description which follows, where the poor starving wretch is represented as almost too far gone to eat and drink the good things Pip has stolen for him.

"He was awfully cold, to be sure. I half expected to see him drop down before my face, and die of deadly

cold. His eyes looked so awfully hungry, too, that when
I handed him the file, and he laid it down on the grass,
it occurred to me he would have tried to eat it if he had
not seen my bundle. 'What's in the bottle, boy?' said
he. 'Brandy,' said I. He was already handing mince-
meat down his throat in the most curious manner—more

COOLING CHURCH BY MOONLIGHT.

like a man who was putting it away somewhere in a
violent hurry than a man who was eating it—but he
left off to take some of the liquor. He shivered all the
while so violently that it was quite as much as he could
do to keep the neck of the bottle between his teeth
without biting it off. 'I think you have got the ague,'

said I. ' I'm much of your opinion, boy,' said he. ' It's bad about here,' I told him. ' You've been lying out on the meshes, and they're dreadful aguish. Rheumatic too.' ' I'll eat my breakfast afore they're the death of me,' said he. ' I'll beat the shivers so far, I'll bet you.' He was gobbling mince-meat, meat-bone, bread, cheese, and pork-pie all at once ; staring distrustfully while he did so at the mist all around us, and often stopping— even stopping his jaws—to listen."—Chap. III.

In Chap. VII. Pip goes to Rochester with Mr. Pumblechook on his way to Miss Havisham's. " I had heard of Miss Havisham up town—everybody, for miles round, had heard of Miss Havisham up town— as an immensely rich and grim lady who lived in a large and dismal house barricaded against robbers, and who led a life of seclusion."

In the tale this is called *Satis House*, but Mr. Forster tells us that *Restoration House* is the one Dickens had in view. I give here, on another page, a view of Restoration House from the Vines, and also a view of the real Satis House as it at present exists. The latter stands on the site of the celebrated mansion, where in the time of Richard Watts Queen Elizabeth was lodged and entertained.

Restoration House is a fine specimen of Elizabethan or Jacobean domestic architecture, and is now the property of Stephen T. Aveling, Esq. ; it seems to have

RESTORATION HOUSE.
The "Satis House" of *Great Expectations.*

SATIS HOUSE, ROCHESTER.

had great attractions for Dickens, and will be referred to again further on.

THE GUILDHALL, ROCHESTER.

In Chap. XIII. Pip is bound apprentice to his good brother-in-law, Joe Gargery, and there is a graphic sketch of the Guildhall with its "shining black portraits on the walls, which my inartistic eye regarded as a composition of hardbake and sticking-plaster."

The Blue Boar in this tale is meant for the Bull Hotel. There is an inn in the High Street with the sign of the Blue Boar, but the description in every particular points to The Bull, and the other sign is probably only introduced to make the locality less easy of identification.

The notable recollections of Dickens in this tale are the convicts and the convict-ships, "like wicked Noah's arks," the ancient city with its suburbs and surroundings, and perhaps, in the childhood of Pip, some tender glimmerings of his own early life.

Of the characters in this book the most easily recognisable as studies from life, are the Old Bailey Attorney with his creaking boots, and his "halo of scented soap;" Mr. Jaggers comes, in point of time, nearly at the end of a long list of lawyers, but he is surely one of the finest descriptive efforts of Charles Dickens. Old Bill Barley, of Mill Pond Bank, too, is a rare example of observation and power of expression in a very few words; no one in the tale had seen this waterside curiosity (except his daughter Clara), but he had been *heard* vibrating in the beam, and "pegging with some dreadful instrument overhead," and he remains as one of the *realities* of the story!

Old Bill Barley and Commodore Trunnion in *Peregrine*

GATEHOUSE OF CATHEDRAL CLOSE, ROCHESTER.

Pickle are so much alike, in speech at least, that we shall probably not err greatly in supposing that Dickens had the Commodore in his mind when he created the gouty old Purser in this tale.

The following passage possibly records a frequent experience of Charles Dickens; in the tale it is the experience of "Pip," after he had for a time realised his expectations :—

" It was interesting to be in the quiet old town once more, and it was not disagreeable to be here and there suddenly recognised and stared after. One or two of the tradespeople even darted out of their shops, and went a little way down the street before me, that they might turn, as if they had forgotten something, and pass me face to face—on which occasions I don't know whether they or I made the most pretence; they of not doing it, or I of not seeing it."

The story of *Great Expectations* lies either in Rochester and neighbourhood, or London, and, like *Edwin Drood*, is so full of Rochester and London that either book might, equally with his terrible story of the French Revolution, have been called *A Tale of Two Cities*.

OUR MUTUAL FRIEND, 1864, cannot be said to contain many recollections of the author's own childhood, but there are in it the sketches of waterside places at the East End of London (places which Dickens had known well as a little boy) which are as good as anything in all his writings.

The ruined windmill mentioned in the story was a conspicuous object on the banks of the Thames fifty years since, and here in this mill Gaffer Hexam "dwelt deep and dark in Limehouse Hole, among the riggers, and the mast, oar, and block makers"—the very spot, in fact, where Dickens' godfather, Christopher Huffam, had formerly carried on a lucrative business (see Chap. III.).

Before proceeding to the last of the books of Dickens, it may be briefly noted here that there are in occasional papers in *Household Words* and *All the Year Round*, other distinct recollections of his own early days ; also in some of the Christmas numbers not previously mentioned, there are many such allusions. They can, however, only be indicated here, and first, in *Household Words* for May 1850, the BEGGING-LETTER WRITER'S horse drops dead at Chatham. This town is also selected for use in THE DETECTIVE POLICE, July 1850, and in ONE MAN IN A DOCKYARD, September 1851, there is besides a description of the "Yard," a fine passage on Rochester Castle, as follows, "What a brief little practical joke I seemed to be, in comparison with its solidity, stature, strength, and length of life."

Then there is THE CHRISTMAS TREE, 1850. "Being at home again, and alone, the only person in the house awake, my thoughts are drawn back, by a fascination which I do not care to resist, to my own Childhood ; "

"Jasper's Gatehouse"
Showing door of "Postern Stair," on the plate of which Mr. Hull
has playfully put the word Jasper.

there are also LYING AWAKE, the beautiful allegorical tale, THE CHILD'S STORY, written in 1852, with its touching, almost prophetic, allusions to events which were to happen in his own family circle, and DOWN WITH THE TIDE. All these shorter pieces are very thoughtfully written, and will repay a very careful reading.

In EDWIN DROOD Charles Dickens was doing some of the best work he had ever done, but like his own life, alas! "it was appointed that the book should shut with a spring for ever and ever." [1]

The surname *Drood* is adapted from that of a Mr. Trood, formerly landlord of the Falstaff Inn, Gad's Hill, and the scene of the tale is laid chiefly in Rochester under the thin disguise of Cloisterham.

In looking through the MS. of this tale in the Forster collection at South Kensington, three things at least are noteworthy. In the first place, as originally written, the first chapter, THE DAWN, opens thus: "An ancient English Cathedral *Town?* How can the ancient English Cathedral *town* be here?" The word Town was afterwards struck out and *Tower* substituted in the printed book.

In the second place it is noticeable that though in this MS. interlineations and corrections abound, yet in Edwin Drood's letter to his uncle John Jasper, the text

[1] *A Tale of Two Cities*, Book I, Chap. III.

runs straight on almost without alteration, and indeed the entire folio of this part of Chap. X. is about the clearest example in the whole MS. This is the more remarkable when we remember that Dickens in one of his letters (written some years before) represents himself as getting on famously with his work, "no blotting, as when writing fiction; but straight on, as when writing ordinary letter" (*Life*, vol. i., p. 20). So thoroughly to the very last did he throw *himself* into his characters, and identify himself *with* his characters.

In the third place this MS. is imperfect; one folio of the opening of the eleventh chapter is missing! It is that portion describing Staple Inn, and the mysterious inscription P. J. T.!

During the writing of *Edwin Drood* Charles Dickens was frequently in Rochester, and was as frequently seen by Mr. Miles the Sacristan, to be studying the Cathedral and its precincts most attentively.

In this tale, though, alas! only a fragment, the solution of the *mystery* is certainly foreshadowed. Jasper (a honoured local name by-the-bye) murders his nephew, Edwin Drood, and it is with reason supposed that, in the end, the crime would have been found to have been committed in the Cathedral itself!

In Chap. XXIII., Jasper, in the incoherent ramblings produced by opium, lets fall a hint or two as to his crime and its inevitable remorse: "A hazardous and perilous journey, over abysses where a slip would be destruction. Look down, look down! You see what lies at the bottom there?" "He is on his feet, speaking in a whisper, and as if in the dark.—No struggle, no consciousness of peril, no entreaty—and yet I never saw *that* before."

THE CRYPT, ROCHESTER CATHEDRAL.
(After a drawing by "Phiz.")

There is in this passage some suggestion of a reason for that strange nocturnal visit to the Cathedral, when Jasper, accompanied by Durdles, climbs the heights of the great tower, and looks down from Triforium and clerestory galleries, as Dickens himself had surely done!

His last visit to Rochester was on Monday the

6th June, 1870, when he walked over from Gad's Hill, accompanied by his dogs. On this occasion he was seen by several persons leaning on the fence in front of Restoration House, and apparently examining the old mansion with great care. It was remarked at the time that there would be some notice of this building in the tale then current, and nothing was more likely, for on the following day, Tuesday, or possibly Wednesday, we find he had in the last chapter of the story ever to be written, reintroduced "the Vines," a fine open space immediately in front of Restoration House.[1]

There is a passage in *Great Expectations*, Chap. XXIX., descriptive of this same house, which seems to have an additional meaning now. " I had stopped to look at the house as I passed, and its seared red-brick walls, blocked windows, and strong green ivy, clasping even the stacks of chimneys with its twigs and tendons, as if with sinewy old arms, made up *a rich attractive mystery*."

Another easily recognisable architectural feature in this work, " The Nun's House," or Eastgate House, is a Ladies' School no longer, but externally, at least, it presents the same appearance as when Dickens was a boy here ; so does the picturesque block of buildings immediately opposite to it, mentioned in the tale as

---

[1] " The Vines " was formerly a vineyard, and it will be noted that in the tale Dickens calls it the Monk's Vineyard.

RESTORATION HOUSE, ROCHESTER.

Mr. Sapsea's premises ; so does the west front of the Cathedral itself, and indeed the entire surroundings of this quiet spot are but little changed in the last fifty or sixty years !

The figure of Mr. Sapsea's father " in the act of

EASTGATE HOUSE, ROCHESTER.

selling " (see initial letter, page 64), which in the story is said to face the Nun's House, was really to be seen some thirty to forty years since over the door of a house in St. Margaret's Banks, Rochester. In times long since passed (practical joking being then a venial offence), several generations of young officers in succession attempted to remove this "wooden effigy," but he was too firmly fixed, and defied all their efforts.

In this story again there is evidence of the results of the early readings at Chatham.

The Princess Puffer (who dealt in opium) asks both Edwin Drood and Mr. Datchery for a specific sum of money, three-and-sixpence, and in each case succeeds in getting it. Mr. Datchery, however, remarks, "Wasn't it a little cool to name your sum? Isn't it customary to leave the amount open? Mightn't it have the appearance, to the young gentleman—only the appearance—that he was rather dictated to?"

In Mrs. Inchbald's *Lovers' Vows*, Act III., Scene I, Baron Wildersheim is asked by a supposed beggar to give him a dollar, and the Baron replies, "This is the first time I was ever dictated to by a beggar what to give him."

My illustrations to this, and some other portions of this book, are from careful drawings by the late William Hull, of Manchester and Rydal, and have been universally admired, as being faithful representations of *Cloisterham* and its antiquities. I shall not be likely to forget the delight of my friend, on taking him a drive from the Bull at Rochester, to Cooling, and Cliffe, and Gad's Hill, nor his having the brougham stopped that he might more closely examine the brilliant effect of some mosses, growing on the reddest of red tiles, on an old building near Cliffe Street.

ROCHESTER CATHEDRAL (WEST DOOR).

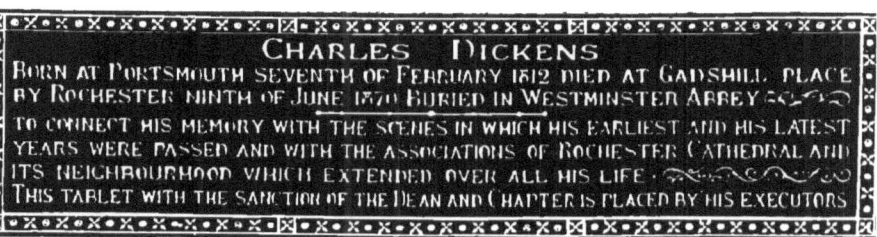

BRASS IN WALL OF SOUTH TRANSEPT, ROCHESTER CATHEDRAL.

"I must come here again, and try and fix some of this wonderful colour next summer," he quietly remarked, as we terminated our visit to Gad's Hill; but, it was not to be for him, before "next summer" came round, he was laid at rest in the quiet churchyard at Grasmere.

Mr. Edward Hull also has, since his brother's death, made many drawings for this work, and especially the views at Cobham, the two Schools of Charles Dickens, the Cedar Trees at Gad's Hill, the Houses at Ordnance Terrace and on the Brook, and a number of interesting views about Chatham and Rochester.

It is most probable, I think, that had Charles Dickens lived to complete *Edwin Drood*, some of the views of *Cloisterham* given here would have been engraved as illustrations to the story.

The tailpiece is from a sketch made on June 9th, 1881 ; the show of wreaths, floral crosses, bouquets, and single flowers, laid on the grave in Westminster Abbey, on the anniversary of the death of Dickens, has, I am assured, been more than maintained since then !

With one short extract (*Edwin Drood*, Chap. XVI.) these retrospective notes may appropriately close ; it has a sad, almost prophetic meaning now. Charles Dickens was telling us of a Christmas Eve in Cloisterham, and he thus beautifully describes what he himself had, no doubt, seen and felt :—

"A few strange faces in the streets ; a few other

faces, half strange and half familiar, once the faces of Cloisterham children, now the faces of men and women who come back from the outer world at long intervals. To these, the striking of the Cathedral clock, and the cawing of the rooks, are like voices of their nursery time.

"To such as these, it has happened in their dying hours afar off, that they have imagined their chamber floor to be strewed with the autumnal leaves fallen from the elm trees in the close : so have the rustling sounds and fresh scents of their earliest impressions revived, when the circle of their lives was very nearly traced, and the beginning and the end were drawing close together."

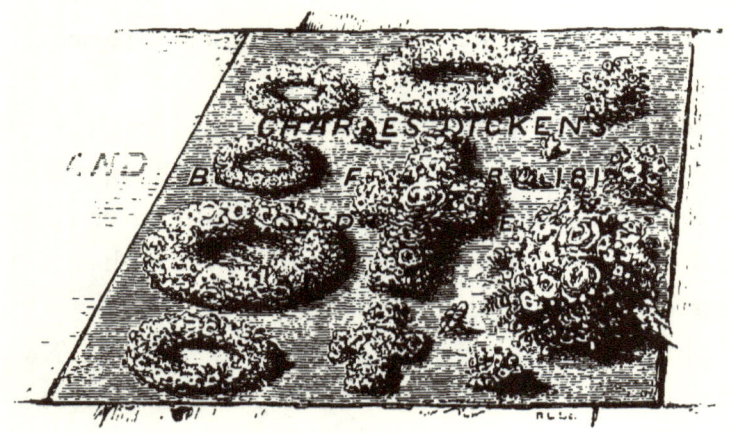

"They" (the flowers) "mark the graves of those who had very tender loving friends."—*Old Curiosity Shop,* Chap. LIV.

THE END.

STROOD HILL, KENT.

INDEX.

S